I dedicate this book to my siblings. Pick up a project that you wanted to start, a goal you wanted to accomplish. Most importantly do not be afraid of failure. Especially the first time around.

To the readers: We all have something that God has gifted us with. First time using it for some, will not produce the desired result. If you polish it, keep evolving it, then you have found your creativity.

Table of Contents

CHAPTER 1

The Beginning

There before a bonfire, sat 6 strangers. You could tell they were travelers just by looking at their rag clothing and the stench they had about them. Many battles they have known. Frequent those battles must have been for them to no longer care about cleaning their weapons. All six of them sat there listening intently to the old man across from them. As the fire glowed and warmed them, they listened with undivided attention to what he was about to say. A long way they have traveled, and the old stranger could be the key to ridden their lands of the evil that plagued it for so long. Taking a sip of water the old man began recounting and sharing his knowledge of what was in the beginning.

"Long, long ago, when darkness and light had equal footing on this earth, there were two siblings. Twins. A man and a woman. Created by God himself, guardians were they; and their tasks were to make sure that darkness never overpowered the earth. For what darkness does best is but consume that which is good. Creating chaos and destruction until nothing that does not resemble it is left standing. How were they to fulfill their task? Their task was a simple one, guarding two wells opposite each other. Of the well of evil, none were to drink; but of the well of light, it was to be freely given to all those who sought wisdom. How did they stop men from drinking from the forbidden well? It was with logic. They persuaded men by words alone. But for it to work, they had to work in unison. Abe provided knowledge as to what the well of evil promises, power, fame, money, kingdoms, as wells as, torment, jealousy, war, hatred, greed, hurt, and self-destruction; Liz, on the other hand, taught the benefits of seeking wisdom. It provided joy, peace, goodness, intelligence, prosperity, and longevity. And that is how they fulfilled their tasks dutifully for centuries.

For centuries indeed, until all together man forgot of their existence and that of the well. On the days they were tempted to leave their post behind and live among the villages of man, the Lord reminded them of their purpose.

"Your purpose is to give to all who come, of the well of light, till no ounce of wisdom remains. For, to all those that have drunk of it, from their bloodlines will I create for myself warriors. Guardians and conquerors that shall fight against the darkness when I set it free. They will fight and win so that all that remains is goodness and peace throughout the lands and times to come."

But Abe who longed after what man had, one fateful night left his sister's side and down the mountain, he went into man's camp. And every night henceforth he would go down and marvel at man's ways and early before sunrise he would leave. In his selfishness and folly, he failed to notice that he was different. Different in speech and different in appearance. And soon enough, mankind got curious and started to follow him up the mountain. When they lost his tracks, they knew he would be back the next day. Sure enough, they, mankind rediscovered the existence of the well. Unbeknownst to Liz, Abe was behind it all. Seeing the wells, the men that came up, five in total, were curious as to what was in them; and why two people would live so far up a mountain by themselves."

"Who are you, people? What business do ye carry up these mountains?" They asked.

"We are guardians." Started Abe. "And our mission is to provide men with wisdom and light with which to face the darkness to come." Finished Liz.

"Behind me is the well of darkness. It promises and gives but never as expected. When it gives, it takes everything from you. None can drink of its waters, nor pry the lid off it." Informed Abe.

"Behind me is the well of wisdom. Drink from it and you will learn to live in peace among your people. Prosperous will you be and with no fear of it being taken from you." Said Liz.

"Peace? Who needs peace? We have plenty of that. We want more. Gives us power and fame and gold! That is what we desire. For what is life if it is not to eat, drink and sleep and on the morrow be no more." Proclaimed the biggest one of the lots.

"All that which you seek my well will grant, but you won't live to enjoy it." Informed Abe.

"Drink from mines, and all that you seek and much more, will you not only find, but you will live an abundant life with which to enjoy them." Said Liz.

At those words, the men who had followed Abe up the mountain started thinking. One of the five, the shortest among them, spoke up and asked, "If what you say is true, why don't you have these things?"

"Yeah" agreed the other 4.

"We are guardians, our sole purpose is to guard these well and to guide mankind toward the well of light. We were never given access to drink of the well I guard." Replied Liz.

"So, if you can't drink from yours, why not drink from his?" the second man questioned Liz.

"The well I guard is total evil. So evil that it cannot stay without a lid. One small drop and it's enough to destroy the peace that you all take oh so lightly." Said Abe.

"How do we know you're not just bluffing? For you two to live up these mountains without proper shelter, you're surely hiding something?" Said the third man in suspicion.

"We assure you," started Liz, "all that we have said is the truth." Finished Abe.

"If that is the case, then what are we waiting for?" Said the fourth man, who among the five seemed the wisest.

"What is your name, good sir?" asked Liz.

"Kalyr, me lady."

"Sir Kalyr, would you like to obtain wisdom? Do you choose to drink of the well of light which is free to all those who come?"

"Without conditions?" asked Kalyr.

"Without conditions nor consequences."

"Aye, me lady."

Stepping forward, Kalyr walked to Liz. With a gesture of the hand, as one giving another permission, Liz gestured at the well. Approaching it, Kalyr could feel strength running through him. Courage. And yet zero fear of caution. Nothing hinting at not to drink this. Picking up the bucket off the rim of well, he lowered it inside. Filling it halfway he drew it back. The bucket now in his grasp, behold it was water.

"Do not be fooled, dear Sir, though it is water, it is much more than that." Said Liz as she could tell what he was thinking.

Without hesitating, Kalyr lifted the bucket against his lips and drunk. His friends, the four that came up with him, waited in silence. Some fear that it was a trap of some sort. The rest thinking, it is all a big joke.

"Kalyr?" called out one of the men.

"I, I don't feel any different." Responded Kalyr as he set the bucket down.

"Wisdom is not apparent in your physic. Wisdom comes in times of need. It is there for you to use whenever the need arises." Assured Liz.

Giving a half bow, Kalyr walked away from Liz and toward his friends.

"How are you feeling?" said one. "Are you feeling any smarter?" asked another.

"Honestly, I feel like myself. I don't feel any different." Responded Kalyr.

"What did you feel when you drank its content?" asked the fourth man. "Cause if you didn't feel anything, I much rather drink from the second well. The well of darkness."

"No Saul, you cannot." Ordered Kalyr to Saul who was contemplating the unthinkable. "Think for a second, if I drank and gained wisdom, what do you think this well will do to you?"

"It'll give me power. It'll give me control." Replied Saul in an envious tone.

Stepping in front of Saul who now was walking toward the well of darkness, "I can't let you do this. You heard what Abe said, it will give you what you want, but it will also take away everything. It gives only to take back."

"Step aside Kalyr. You drank what you wanted, now let me drink of my choice." Demanded Saul.

"No brother I cannot." Said Kalyr with a voice of plea.

"Zig? Are you with me?" Asked Saul as he turned to look at one of the three men present, seeking support.

Zig was the one who questioned Liz on drinking from her brothers well. Walking toward Saul, putting a hand on his shoulder he said, "I know you're the biggest among us, not just in size, in years also, but I am with Kalyr on this one. If we can be sure of one thing it is that, that well which you lust after, it is sealed for a reason. I'd pass on this one if I were you."

Saul disappointed turned around and looked at the remaining two men there, "Teo and Leo?" Teo was the shortest one among them; and Leo was the one who questioned if what the guardians were saying was not a bluff. Looking back at Saul they nodded. A nod that meant, 'we're with you on this.' Taking a final look at Kalyr and Zig, he and both Teo and Leo left the mountain top and headed back to the village below.

"Thank you Zig," Kalyr said in recognition of his support.

"No need to thank me, Kal. Just look at it. Just the sheer sight of it, says death. I don't know what you drank in that well, but I sure as hell will not drink from Abe's." Said Zig as he stared at it.

"Sir Kalyr, will you be bringing more people up this mountain to gain wisdom?" Asked Liz.

"I don't believe that that would be a good idea. I feel fate brought me up here, just as I am sure, fate also brought all those who were before me. Well, to be honest, I always wanted to explore these mountains top. So eventually I would have stumbled upon you. But I think the reason why I came sooner, well, we came sooner, is because your..." Kalyr was interrupted by Abe.

"What matters now is that you are here. You made the right choice, that's what counts." Said Abe.

Understanding that Abe wanted to hide his adventures down the mountain a secret, Kalyr said no more. With a concerned look on his face, he looked at Abe, "Saul will be back. He is a stubborn one, and he will not stop until he sees the content of the well you guard. So, for tonight, Zig and I will stay here."

That night both Zig and Kalyr slept on the mountain top. Kalyr stayed close to Liz who recounted all her adventures with those who came up. Of all the things she could hear happening down below in the camps of man; and how she longed to see what they see and be in their presence. Zig on the other hand was stuck staring at Abe's well, since sunset to nightfall.

"Interesting, don't you think? It's a beautiful mystery it holds don't you think?" Abe asked Zig as he interrupted his stare.

"There is nothing beautiful about it. At best it's disgraceful." Replied Zig.

"Disgraceful? How so?"

"For starters, it's forbidden. Second, it destroys even that which you have. There is no way that whatever is in there can have any trait of beauty. Honestly, I wish I never knew of your existence. But now because of you, we're stuck up here helping you guard whatever abomination rest inside of this sealed well." Blamed Zig.

"And we appreciate it very much." Said Abe.

Looking at Abe, Zig's stare said it all. It was a stare that condemned. A stared of unbelief. One that said, 'if anything happens now because you came down to us, it's all on you.' Turning his back to Abe he got up and went to Kalyr and Liz. "You know something Liz," Zig said as he got close, "Kalyr doesn't have a wife. He doesn't have any children either."

Hushing Zig away, Kalyr pulled a handful of grass and threw it at him. "Don't pay attention to what he's saying. It is without importance." Reassured kalyr.

"Yeah, sure. Guess who's going to be heading down the mountain saying, they 'think they are in love?'" Teased Zig.

"Zig!" yelled Kalyr after him.

"Alright, Alright. What do you guys eat up here?" asked Zig, changing the subject.

"Oh, I can show you. We have an array of tree bearing fruits. Follow me right this way!" offered Abe.

"What about pooping? Where do you guys go?" Zig was heard asking as Abe led the way.

"My friend, some questions are best left unanswered." Responded Abe.

CHAPTER 2

Evil Set Free

Turning back to Liz, Kalyr could see that she understood every last one of Zig's commentary about a wife, kids, and love. She was blushing. She was blushing because that too she could hear among men from where she was, and always wondered what it was like. What it is like to be married, to have children, to love, and then die.

Changing the subject, Kalyr asked, "so, what is there to be seen from up here?"

"To be seen?" questioned a puzzled Liz

"Yeah, like is there a waterfall, a hidden glowing lake, or something? An unknown creature? My question is, what is your favorite thing to do up here?"

"Ah, I see. Well, I do not know. There is a lake to the left of my well behind the tree lines, but it does not glow. There is a waterfall over at the bottom of that hill to your right however, you probably don't want to go diving in; it is the one that falls at the foot of the mountain."

"Yeah, let's not do that."

"But my favorite thing to do is to watch the night's sky." Admitted Liz.

"What's so special about that? I gaze at it often when I am down..." Kalyr responded but stopped once he looked up. "Wow, they're bigger. The stars are bigger!"

"Yep! Sometimes I get lost in thought just looking at them." Said Liz as she admired the stars. "Kalyr, the stars are up there, not my face."

"You're right. The stars are not on your face. But from what I can see, the stars aren't the only beauty worth admiring tonight." Boldly said Kalyr. Liz was blushing uncontrollably, though Kalyr could not tell since she turned her face away from him.

Unbeknownst to the two, someone was slowly closing in on them from behind. The intruder was ever so silent. So, light on his feet was he that he now knelt behind in between Liz and Kalyr. "So," said the man, as he interrupted the romantic atmosphere, "has he asked you to marry him yet?" Said Zig as he hurriedly ran from Kalyr.

"Zig!" yelled a startled Kalyr, "really, you just can't help yourself, can you?" Said he as he chased Zig down the garden he just came from.

Chasing Zig, Kalyr stumbled upon Abe who now was chuckling at the situation. "Abe, where did he go?" For Zig was a fast runner. The fastest you could say.

"Straight ahead!" Exclaimed Abe. And with that, Kalyr took off after him. He of course would in no way harm Zig. They had been friends since childhood.

Nearing his sister Abe asked Liz in a normal tone at first, "Did tell him that you're immortal?"

"No, I didn't. But I think he already figured that out," answered Liz.

"You know they can't stay up here, don't you? Especially Kalyr. He'll distract you from your task." Retorted a bitter Abe. Bitter, because her sister had found something he could not without leaving the mountain top. Bitter, that she was satisfied with just this moment even if it did not last long. Bitter that she could have so little yet be content. Bitter that, she got more attention than he did. That his well was sealed shut and none could drink from it, yet from hers, it was freely given and encouraged.

So jealous was he that his emotions started stirring the darkness that laid in the well. So stirred was it that the dark forces that were sipping their presence into their known world. The borders of the well glowed a darkish red. Kalyr who was still trying to catch Zig sensed something was wrong. Looking back toward where he left Liz and Abe, he had this growing feeling of fear, anger, and death. Without a second's notice, he ran back. Zig, who was hiding in the bushes, seeing the look on his friend's face, knew something was up. The only time he ever had such a look on his face was 5 years ago when Kalyr's wife was pregnant. They were out hunting when it happened. When his wife died. She died in labor with the child. But Kalyr, he sensed her distress, he sensed something was wrong. The look on his face then was the same as the one he has on now. Without wasting any more time, Zig ran after him. Having traveled deep within the mountain terrain, they had a long way to go.

"What do you sense?" asked Zig as he caught up to his friend.

"I don't know exactly, but I sense death. I fear a battle will be waiting for us. One with grave consequences. We got to hurry." Replied Kalyr.

"I am a faster runner, I'll run up ahead and stall the situation. I would not be surprised if this were the doing of Saul. See ya!" said Zig as he ran before Kalyr.

"Saul? Wait, if this is his doing then you can be sure he will not be alone. WAIT ZIG, do not go alone. ZIG! ZIG!" yelled an out of breath Kalyr.

Zig did indeed hear Kalyr, but his warning was not what concerned him the most. What did was two folds. The first being the well of darkness and making sure, Saul did not have access to it. The second being to protect Liz not just from Saul but from Abe. The little time he spent with him in the forest, he could tell he was envious of her. And if that well came close to being unsealed Abe would not lift a finger in stopping that from happening, leaving Liz to defend it herself which would lead to untold and unfavorable results and consequences. "You were robbed in the past Kalyr. I won't let it happen again." Said Zig as he made haste.

In the meantime, Liz was conversing with Abe. "Abe, just because I don't say anything, doesn't mean I don't know about your habitual walks down the mountain. Your ambition and greed have doomed us all and you are the only one to blame. I hope you can live with the consequences of your actions."

Abe was stupefied. He was at a loss for words, but not in lack of anger. He was fuming at the realization that Liz knew and said nothing. That she did not try to dissuade him.

"In case you're wondering why I never stopped you," Liz continued, "you are responsible for your actions, just as I am of mine. But above all, you are responsible for guarding your well as I am for my own. Your will is something you're in control of. Countless times, have I encouraged you to not give up; that though we do not understand God's purpose, our duties remained the same. But you chased after your desires, and now, what must happen will happen."

"WHAT? WHAT WILL HAPPEN? HAVE YOU FORESEEN THIS? WHAT IS TO HAPPEN?" Questioned a furious Abe.

"You will soon find out." Replied a faint-hearted Liz as she got up and went and stood beside her well. No sooner than she got there that Saul came out of the bushes with Teo and Leo wielding swords. Having had his back to the bushes, he heard movement behind him. Turning around he saw the three men coming toward them. Trying to regain his composure he walked in their direction thinking it would be just as before. Persuade through words. That was far from the truth. Without hesitating, as soon as Saul was within arm's reach of Abe, he slashed at him with an upward swing of his sword striking him across the chest. Shock at what just happened, Abe stood still as pain rushed across his torso and chest. All he could do was watch as his blood ran down his clothes and the three intruders walked past him toward Liz.

Seeing what occurred before her, Liz was scared but not surprised. She dared not move from where she stood. She knew something like this would have eventually happened. It was just a matter of time. Waiting for her turn, she stood boldly. Raising his sword as he neared her, Saul was walking decisively. He was a man with one goal in mind, kill, and not be persuaded otherwise. No time to give ear to reasoning, strike first to win, to rob, to steal. Standing before Liz, he took one last look at her before swinging his sword for a fatal blow. Liz could see the other two men, Teo and Leo smirking and laughing in the background behind Saul, encouraging the outrage, the sin, the murder. Closing her eyes, she awaited the strike, the pain, and the numbness to follow.

Being so sure of themselves, they all failed to notice Zig, coming in from their left. Without hesitating, without a moment's notice, Saul was tackled to the ground. It happened so fast. One moment Saul was before their eyes, before Teo and Leo, and the next he was not. So violent was the tackle, so powerful the push, so swift the defense that both men landed several meters from Liz and the others. So determined was Zig that he knew of the three present, Saul would have to be the first to be taking care of. Being bigger than himself, his only chance of succeeding against Saul was in striking first. And first, he did. His strength and force behind the tackle broke two of Saul's ribs, sending him rolling in pain.

So quick was Zig, that he had time to get back up, grab Saul's sword, and face the other two opponents before they realized what happened. Turning to their right, Teo and Leo started to comprehend what had happened. Their laughter and smirk turned to utter hatred as they ran after Zig. Zig, being the fastest of them, easily subdue them. Teo charged in sword up in the air, rendering it easy for Zig to parry his attack and plunge his sword in him. Leo came in with a jab of the sword that Zig also easily parried and fatally struck his once known companion. "You guys asked for it. It didn't have to be this way." Said a sadden Zig as he watched the men pass away.

Thinking he was done, Zig turned around to finish what he had started. Saul was still on the floor but had made the effort to get up on his knees. His eyes contained only hatred. A hatred that wanted nothing more than to destroy. "I am glad Kalyr won't be here to see me like this. He has had to keep you out of trouble for far too long. After today, he'll be able to go on and live his life." Those were Zig's words as he readied the sword for a sweeping motion to finish off the foe he now stood before.

Standing still steadying his sword, Zig felt two stings on his back. They were simultaneous. And slowly and speedily the sting grew into intense pain. Reaching for his back, Zig knew exactly what he was touching. He was struck with arrows. Turning around he could see 10 more men coming from the bushes.

"I hope you didn't think I would've come back here in small numbers," said Saul as he struggled to speak due to his pain, but yet managed to let out a smirk.

"Nah, I don't think. I just prepare for the worst." And with that response, Zig kicked Saul in his rib cage, breaking new bones, and plunging the already broken bones into his vital organs. "You can't die a quick death I just realized. Yours must be an agonizing one. I am not Kalyr, but soon you'd wish I were." Said he as he walked away from suffering Saul. Taking a glance at Liz he gestured for her to take cover behind the well before running toward the new threats.

By the time Kalyr arrived the battle was already over and the first thing he saw as he got near was the body of Leo and Teo. Followed by the sight of Zig's body lying on the floor and Liz sitting next to him. Looking past Liz, he saw Saul making his way for her with a weapon in hand.

"SAUL!!" yelled out Kalyr as he ran toward him. At the sheer sight of Kalyr Saul was frightened. Zig was a formidable foe, more formidable than Kalyr. But when Kalyr is angry Zig gets outclassed. So scared was Saul of Kalyr that he abandoned his quest to go after Liz and contended to save his life. Being in so much pain and having a perforated lung, all he could do was drag his feet and weight off the ground as fast as he could and as much as he could endure.

Seeing him flee, Kalyr contended to stay by Liz's side. "Are you alright? You're not hurt, are you?"

"No, no I am fine. Zig protected me from them." Replied Liz.

Inspecting her, there was not a single drop of blood on her except for her hands. "Wait your hands are...?"

"No that's not my own, that's Zig's," reassured Liz.

"Zig? Hey Zig?" Said Kalyr as he gently touched him, to see if there would be a response. "Zig?" Said he, as he watched his friend lay on his side.

"Oh, now you remember me don't ya? I always knew you would abandon our friendship for a woman." Joked Zig.

"This is not the time to joke around Zig," Said Kalyr, "you're bleeding."

"Am I?" Questioned Zig. "What happened?"

"Come on Zig, seriously lay off the humor, now's not the time." Complained Kalyr.

"He was struck with two arrows in the back. I pulled them out when he fell unconscious."

"I, fell unconscious? Me? No way!" exclaimed Zig.

"You did. Right after you were hit in the head with this branch." Said Liz as she pointed to branch laying on the ground above his head. The man who struck you with it ran for his bow and arrow. Which is why I ran to cover you. But, as soon as Kalyr showed up he took off." Informed Liz.

"How many men got away?" Asked Zig.

"Just that one man, and Saul's here struggling to escape." Said she as they all looked at him in pity.

"Well, as long as we're alive, that's what counts..." Zig was cut off.

"Hello?! You were shot with two arrows and you're not concerned that you'll bleed out?" asked a furious Kalyr.

"Not really. I live, I live, I die, I die. Just kidding. I am wearing my armor. Although I must say they did pierce through a little. So, I am not surprised by the bleeding, just that it is not a mortal wound," reassured Zig as he groaned. "I am getting old. I did too much moving around. Kalyr, you need to start doing your part. You are getting sloppy and lazy. How could you leave the protection of such a lovely woman in my care?" Joked Zig.

"Only you Zig. Only you." Replied an unbelieving Kalyr. "Speaking of you, where's Abe?"

"Abe? I forgot about him. He was right... there..." said Zig as he pointed toward the spot, he last saw him. Looking around, he saw him behind the well of darkness about to undo the seal. "ABE DON'T!" yelled Zig. That's where Kalyr and Liz turned their gaze to see what Zig was responding to.

Without hesitating, Kalyr bounced off the floor and went into a full spring after Abe. For some unknown reason, Kalyr knew if those seals came undone, mankind would be in peril. This evil in that well must be kept locked away. Managing to make it half-way, yet too late, for all hell broke loose. The seal came undone and a bursting gust of wind, having the well at its center sent both, Abe and Kalyr flying backward. Immediately thereafter a cloud of smoke came gushing out, turning night into a reddish glow. And out of that smoke came the most disturbing tone of voice. One, all who heard it would run away from. One, just by the sound alone brought terror. A tone of voice that echoed death. "Free at last. Free. Free. Free."

Rallying himself back toward Liz and Zig, Kalyr picked up a sword and spear with which to face this seemingly immortal threat.

"To whom do we owe our freedom?" Said the smoke looking at the three. "Hmm, you guys seem too pure to have been that stupid to set us free. Especially you, with those threatening eyes," giggles the voices in the smoke as it looked at Kalyr. "Best keep our eyes on you. Who knows what you're capable of." Turning around, it spotted Saul, crawling away. "Not so fast little one," said the voices as they covered Saul in total darkness. As the cloud of smoke cleared, it had condensed itself around him and was able to lift Saul in the air. "Now, there's a wicked heart we can recognize. Surely it must have been you who set us free. You, humans, are so weak. We knew it would not be long before one or several of you gave into lust and greed. And thanks to you, we can now consume everything," sounded the voices in contentment as their tone of speech grew deeper and darker.

"Let me go, you filth! Let me go. I was not the one that set you free. AH!" replied a scared Saul as he suffered a world of pain as he was being squeezed. Coughing up blood, he knew even if he managed to survive, he would not live to see the dawn of day. "What the heck," said he as he knew death awaited, "what have you got to offer?" asked a hurting Saul.

"Offer? We? Ha, ha, ha, foolish human. We don't give anything. All we do is but consume all that you've worked hard to get. Your life, your loved ones, your crops, your herds. We consume all that comes seeking power. We feed off the darkness of men's souls. And tonight, after a very long time, yours is the first we shall have.

Being up against such a threat, Liz, Zig, and Kalyr could only watch as Saul was swallowed inside the dark smoke, with nothing to be found that he ever existed.

"OH, of course, my meal wasn't the one who set us free. Isn't that right Abe?" Said the voices out of the smoke as their tone became one.

"You, you know my name?" questioned Abe.

"Of course, we know your name. You who have been guarding and dissuading men from seeking us, how could we not? Being imprisoned within that well never stopped us from influencing men's hearts. But you two would always dissuade them from setting us free. We knew it would only be a matter of time before the wickedness of men's hearts grew to a degree where words would not suffice. OH, we knew. And now that we are free, we can do much more than just incline the heart to the darkness. We will enslave you to it. We will pave the way and watch you destroy yourselves. And once the evilness of your hearts increases, we'll feast. We will feast through sickness, wars, famines, deaths, hatred, and murder. Oh, what a feast indeed. And we will keep doing so till there is nothing left. From village to village. Islands to Islands. And you Abe shall be at the center of it all to witness your foolishness." Said the entities of smoke. "Where Abe shall live to see his foolishness, you three shall live to help us accomplish it," said the immortal threat to Liz, Kalyr, and Zig.

"We will never help you," Said Liz. "I would rather die than to align myself with you," retorted Zig.

"Oh, that we know. We know it very well. Which is why we aren't asking for permission. We take by force. You three are perfect to house all of us."

"House all of you?" questioned Liz as repeating it started making sense to her. "No, no, I refuse. I refuse to..." Looking at Kalyr and without hesitating, she passed down her aura undo them. It was a veil of light. As her aura left her, it flowed over and enveloped Kalyr and Zig completely. And though that veil looked physically possible to touch, it was not.

"No! Yelled Kalyr and Zig. "What are you doing? What about you?" as they realized what she was doing. Liz removed from herself a portion of her immortality. Her divine protection of long life and against dark forces and passed it onto the two. "The clock now ticks, it's up to the two of you to put an end to what's about to happen," said Liz.

Zig, looking at Kalyr, knew the hurt and anger he was now experiencing. He saw it on his face, the day his wife and child died. And now today, he was witnessing it again. Twice now has he witnessed his best friend shed tears. *"Twice too many,"* thought he. "Stop Liz, stop. You are not protecting yourself. There have to be other options," yelled Zig.

"There isn't." Said Kalyr as he turned to Zig with teary eyes.

"What are you blabbering and plotting? Whatever you think you are doing will not work. We're much, much stronger than you." Declared the shadow as it reached down to grab Kalyr and Zig. Morphing itself into the shape of a giant human, it reached down with its smoky hands to grab them. As soon as its fingers came into contact with the protection that Liz was passing unto the boys, its fingers violently evaporated. As if to say it was annihilated. Angry and in shock and realizing what Liz was doing could mean an end to its newfound freedom he went after her. Forming a fist, he tried to crush her to the ground. Fortunately, the boys were fast enough to jump in and cover her, causing the evil before them to lose both hands.

"We will not be defeated so easily." Said it as it disperses into smoke and causing great darkness to befall them as it swarms around them. And in the cover of that darkness, they grabbed Liz from underneath the boys and wasting no time, went to work on possessing her. As they took possession of her body, the darkness that surrounded them grew faint, till Zig and Kalyr could see what was happening; and before they could get to her, the evil now within Liz grew wings and took off with her.

"And that's the last I saw of her," said the aging man before the group of traveling warriors.

"What happened afterward?" questioned one of the travelers.

"After it took off with her, the ground started rumbling under our feet and a greater cloud of shadow escaped from the well. Except this was different. It did not clutter as the first one did. Instead, it dispersed and fled in many directions. We soon understood that the evil that escaped, that took off with Liz were the leaders, generals I call them. And the ones after were the soldiers. So, for the remainder of our days, Zig and I set out eliminating the soldiers to get to the generals. And wherever we found men willing to align with our cause, we brought them to the well of life and gave them to drink. But they never quite lived as long as we did. I think Liz somehow, passed down some of her immortality to us."

"What happened to Abe?" questioned the same traveler.

"Once we left the mountain top, we never saw him again. We hated him for what he did. I hated him for what happened then, and what happened afterward especially."

"Afterwards?" asked the quietest of the lot.

"Well, I lost my best friend, that's what happened. The task before us proved too great. The second wave of evil that had escaped the well, fled to distant lands. They somehow took control of wild beasts and changed their very nature. And so, because of that, we decided to split up. We split up and our task was to gather as many able fighting men as possible and bring them to the well. I stayed in this land and he traveled to distant ones across the sea. Miraculously enough we had gathered the same number of fighters. Fifty-thousand able men. Men who witnessed the destruction of evil and wanted to put an end to it. Heading up the mountain, which you see behind you, we headed to the well. But upon nearing it, it was dry. The only water that remains is the one you see around my neck. This disappointment in itself wasn't dangerous until he spoke up."

"He?" questioned the first traveler.

"Abe. He accused me and my men of having gone to the well and emptying it till nothing was left. He said we were working with the shadows and only called the warriors across the seas out of their lands so it could fall prey to evil. And before Zig and I could bring to reason the men from across the seas an arrow was shot that mortally wounded one of my men. And a battle ensued. We had no choice but to fight. It was as if everybody had gone mad. It was the same blood lust I'd witness with Saul and his men back then."

"What happened to Zig? Did he die?" asked another among the six.

"Oh no, there was no way he would die so easily. When the battle ended, we were the only two survivors. I think, because of what happened, because it was one of his men that caused us such defeat, he felt guilty of it. I have not seen him again since. And Abe, well, he disappeared once again. I haven't seen him either."

"But why did he do that? What was his goal?" asked the shortest of the travelers.

"I still don't know to this day. But I feared that evil took complete control over his heart." Finished the old man.

"Then it would appear, sir, that the fight is not yet over. For this same evil which you witness and fought still exists in our lands. This is the story that we have been told of sir. We know that four hundred years ago, there was a battle a great battle that took place in our lands. Leading the charge against the forces of darkness were 10 men we have come to call descendants. Heirs of the mission of those like you, sir, that sought to end the reign of darkness once and for all. The witch, as we have grown to call her, was in charge of the forces of evil. At her side, she possessed and controlled ten dragons. Turning against her, they sided with the descendants and locked her up inside of this barrier. A barrier which now is failing. One only needs to approach it to feel the fear on the other side. We can only imagine what wicked being she gave life to, these so many centuries. And this is why we need your help, sir." Recounted the first traveler.

"Well then my sons, these bones could surely use some greasing." Spoke the elderly man as he got up from his chair and slowly stood straight.

"One final battle sir, one final battle." Advanced the man among the travelers who seemed to be the leader of the five. "Help us end it." Said he as he extended his hand toward the elderly man as a sign of alliance.

CHAPTER 3

Present Day

Entering camp during dawn and making their way toward the end of the rows of tents, King Bervard and the men that were with him. As he passed the soldiers that were already there, stood and bow in reverence. Raising his right hand and holding the saddle of his horse with his left hand, he saluted his knights.

"How fair was your battle with the creatures of the land my Lord?" asked a messenger soldier as he walked alongside the king's horse.

"Fair it wasn't for them my lad. The men with me barely broke a sweat." Replied the king.

"Aye, as suspected my Lord, I knew it wouldn't be long till we rid ourselves of them." Returned the messenger.

"How is it with thee?" asked the cheery king as he could see his men had been hard at work. Blacksmiths were already busy at work in the early hours of the morning, sharpening swords and spears and at their foot sat the remnants of iron-tipped arrows. Other soldiers got busy setting up tents for the newcomers to rest. The bowmen were busy target practicing as well as the spear garrison behind the tree lines. It was a beautiful chilled morning in the middle of the woods. The air was much fresher than in the capital.

"It is well with us sire. Although we did lose some men against the one-eyed giants," informed Edwin the messenger.

"How many, my boy?" asked the king

"Twelve my Lord. And against the fast runner, we counted thirty and rising." continued Edwin.

"And rising?" questioned the king. "Did you not capture it as I was told?"

"We did capture it, sire. We had many casualties and among them, some succumbed to their wounds." Said Edwin the messenger.

"God be with them. Brave lots they were." mourned the king.

"Indeed sir! Shall I tell General Philip to meet you in your tent Sire?" Edwin asked of the king, knowing they probably had a lot to inform the other about.

"Yes, please do. Where is he by the way?" asked the king curiously.

"I believe that he's keeping an eye on the beast, my lord," replied Edwin.

"Very well then, tell him I'll come to him once the men and I rest. Four months of scouting we did, throughout the land. Peaceful now it is. And perfect will it be once the last beast is slain." Declared the king.

"We're glad to have you with us sire. Good rest my lord." Said the messenger as he stopped walking, bowed, and allowed the king to continue on his way. Walking straight across the path the king and his company passed through, he entered the forest in search of Philip. He could not believe that it has been four months since they started their quest to rid their kingdom and border of the hideous beasts of darkness. He just like the king and everybody else wondered how they managed to break away from their prison, the dark forest. That forest was supposed to be a prison to some ancient evil, and yet they were able to escape. The royal family no doubt knew the legend in full, otherwise, the way the outposts were positioned around the forest, a way to signal to the entire kingdom that danger was set loose, would not have been so.

Nearing the middle of the forest, the messenger's thoughts were interrupted by the sound of that howling beast. Searching for Philip among the soldiers, he found him keeping watch on the four-legged beast. Distinguishable as always, thought the messenger of the general. He, general Philip, was the one who trained him when he joined the scout regiment. Every regiment in the kingdom was trained in every art of combat but excel at one art. This was so that, in the event of war, one must always be prepared to use whichever weapon was available, if his own broke. There was five art of combat, bow, spear, sword, ax, and shield. The shield division being fairly new, was created to block and counter the attacks of the beasts that escaped the dark forest. He, the messenger was an excellent bowman. But not good enough to lead a regiment. That task was given to those who could master two forms of combat or more. Besides the King and the Philip, there were only five outside of the castle guards with such skills. Five Lieutenant Generals. And the castle guards, boy were they good. Excel at every art and able to take down any foe. Death they feared not. A good battle with unfair odds against them, do they like.

Approaching his superior, the messenger spoke up. "Have you found any weaknesses yet general?" said the messenger referring to the beast.

"No, not yet Edwin. Although it is trying to break free of our hooks, it's not showing any openings in its stance. There is more to this beast than meets the eye. It is a fast runner; we have established that fact. One moment, as we are chasing it in the forest, it was on our left, the next on our right. It is fast, too fast. We cannot take any chances. More hooks!" ordered the general. And with that single order, two archers aimed at the beast's outer hind legs and shot hook tip arrows. The sudden pain caused the beast to yell even louder than before, echoing its voice throughout the forest. Loud was it that the king heard it in his tent as well as the men surrounding him.

"I won't delay my message any longer then," said the messenger. Straightening himself up, he said, "The king and company have arrived. He said he would get some rest before coming out to meet you."

"I see," said Philip. "Brother has arrived at last. How was his journey?" asked the general of his messenger.

"Nothing but successes said he. The only beast left is this one." Paraphrase the messenger.

"Well, that's good. Since the sun is rising, I might as well get some rest. Knowing brother, he will probably want to fight it as soon as he wakes up. Robert and John are out of the question since they've just arrived as well." said Philip as he was pondering out loud whom to keep watch on the beast in his absence.

"What's that general?" asked the messenger.

"Don't mind me, I'm looking for someone to keep watch while I rest," replied Philip

"Ah, I see. I think Smith is awake. Not sure about Black." answered Edwin the messenger.

"My boy if Black was awake, the whole camp would know." Replied the general.

"That's true. Shall I then get Smith then?" asked Edwin.

"Please do. Tell him to be as ruthless as he wants with the beasts and if anything arises then he is to call for me at once. This beast has yet to show us what it's capable of." Ordered Philip.

"Right away general." Said the messenger as he left in search of Smith. Smith was an excellent spearman and a regiment lieutenant general. He was one of the five that could wield and use more than one form of weapon. His second favorite was the ax. With these two in hand, he did not need a shield. Blocking with his ax and attacking with his spear. And in case of 'dire emergency', as he always says, he carries a bow, in the event that he would be too far away from the king to provide protection.

Entering Smith's tent, Edwin found no one in. *"Must be out on his morning rituals,"* thought the messenger, referring to the lieutenant habits of emptying his bowels first thing in

the morning. Sitting down, at the entrance of the tent he
waited for him.

CHAPTER 4

Smith

Edwin, had been waiting for about ten minutes, happened to spot Smith coming from the tree lines, on the opposite side of the forest. *"As discreet as always,"* thought the messenger. Smith was an unusual one, he always had his armor on, even when sleeping.

"You can never be too careful lieutenant general." Edwin greeted Smith, using the man's favorite line.

"Aye, my boy. One must be prepared for everything." Replied Smith. "By the way, how many times must I tell you to just call me lieutenant. Lieutenant general is a mouth full."

"Aye sir, my apologies lieutenant," acknowledge Edwin.

"Now that's better." replied a satisfied Smith as he fixed the waistline of his pants.

"How do you ever manage to go about your business in all this armor? Surely you must take it off on some days, don't you?" asked Edwin.

"Boy, if ever you saw a man in his most intimate moment," referring to the time a man wants peace and quiet, as he empties his bowels, "if you ever saw me in my intimate moment, I'd have to kill you."

"Why?" argued Edwin. "I mean what, you have some sort of scar under that armor that you try to hide?"

"Why are you here messenger?" asked Smith, changing the subject.

"General Philip is going to get some rest, and he requested that you take watch of the runner. And that you'd be without mercy of the beast if required." Informed Edwin as he got up from the ground.

"Sounds like a good morning exercise. Speaking of the beast, how many of our men did it kill?"

"Last I was informed, thirty, sir. Why?"

"For those thirty, I shall inflict the beast with thirty arrows. And if more die, then more arrows it will have to endure."

"What if you end up killing it, sir? The king would surely want to fight it in battle."

"If it dies, it dies, I would have avenged my brethren. Now leave, go wake up Black, and have him join me!" Ordered Smith.

"Right away. Also, not part of the message but speaking of the king, he arrived a little half an hour ago."

"Were Robert and John with him?"

"They were Sir," confirmed Edwin.

"Good, now we can finish our challenge," mumbled Smith to himself.

"Challenge? Sir?" asked a puzzled Edwin as he tried to make sense of what Smith mumbled to himself.

"Nothing my boy!" Exclaimed a joyous Smith. Looking up at the sky, then at the rising sun, his demeanor changed. While still gazing at the rising sun he said, "Looks like today will be a day like none other Edwin. Make full use of it and get some rest yourself."

"Aye, sir." Responded Edwin. *"I wonder what type of challenge he was talking about?"* thought the messenger to himself. Shrugging it off, he went away heading toward his tent. Passing through the camp, he found that it got a lot busier. *"Of course, it would, there's more of us now,"* he answered himself. Of the soldiers that came with the king, some were busy, counting their tales of adventures to friends and comrades. Some were fast asleep in their tents; others laid their tired back against a tree. *"And to think four months ago, we were itching for adventures, and now we just want to go home. Back to our villages, back to the castle, to wife and kids, to brother, to mother and father. We were all tired. Just one more beast to slay and we can go home,"* thought Edwin as he made his way toward his shared tent and flopped himself to sleep on his makeshift cot.

"Morning general." greeted Smith to a tired yet valiant Philip.

"Having a rough morning I see," says Philip, referring to Smith late morning start. "Think you'll last the day without moving from this position?"

"I'll manage. Edwin briefed me that you are going to get some rest. If you are that worried about the king facing this beast, you must have some serious suspicion about it." said Smith.

"I do. Just look at it. For one, it is not trying to break away from the chains. It is showing signs of struggle, but it is as if it wants to be here. Two, you would think with all these hook tip arrows piercing its body It would stop moving and lay still in pain, but no. It is like it does not even feel extreme pain. Just fresh ones, then it is gone. Three, when we were chasing it through the forest, it ...." Philip was interrupted by Smith.

"The way it kept on disappearing?" questioned Smith as he cut off Philip.

"Not only that. It was jumping from position through position." Revealed Philip.

"Please explain?" asked Smith.

"It looked as if it was jumping from formation to formation. The way we had our men fan out through the forest to find and capture it. It went from formation to the next, deliberately so without fear of getting captured or killed. Almost as if, it was looking for ...."

"Someone." Finished Smith. "So, if it was in search of someone, do you think everything else was a diversion?"

"Diversion?" Questioned Philip. "The lesser beats to roam the lands and the bigger ones to travel it through the forest, hidden from sight." said an enlightened General. "Stay put, I shall inform the king," ordered Philip to Smith. "You there," yelled him at a nearby soldier, "get me Black and Sirius and bring them here to Smith."

"Aye Sir!" responded the soldier. *"There goes our morning peace,"* thought the soldier at the task of having Black awake.

"So," softly whispered Smith to himself while looking at the beast, "you and your group were scouts, hein. If you and those one-eyed club-wielding giants are what comes after the beasts the king faced in the fields, what must come after you I wonder? Thirty of our men died, how many more will if that barrier falls?" Smith could have sworn the beast understood every word he said. As soon as he was done talking the four runner, as they have come to name it, looked his way and looked as if it had a smirk on its face. "Interesting," said a cautious Smith, as he tightened his grip on his spear.

Walking as fast and composed as he could with a stern concerned look on his face, Philip walked toward his brother's tent. He could not understand why he did not make sense of the situation earlier. If he was right, that meant that the king was in danger since there was more at work behind the scenes than just dark beasts. An ancient evil was pulling every string. Strings that should never have left the dark forest, her prison. And if history spoke true, that such evil exists, that would mean that the guardians were once alive, as well as them. Them, the descendants granted powers by the kings of all beasts. They were the heir to the power that kept this evil and her kind imprison. Power passed down from generation through generation. Stopping dead in his tracks, he thought, *"How could I be so stupid. If they hold the key and the power to keep her lock. That would mean with them dead, she would be free. So, the king isn't the only one they are after?"* Thought Philip, wondering what the best course of action would be.

CHAPTER 5

The Three

Making his way toward Black's tent, Edwin peered his head inside. Having noticed Lieutenant General John, he hesitated his entrance. John was now the most lenient among the lieutenants. Spotting Robert's boots on the other side of the bed, he did not know what to do. If he tried to wake up Black, it was certain that he risks waking up John as well. And lieutenant John was not the easygoing type with punishments. As he was contemplating taking his chances to go in, a soldier approached him from behind.

"Excuse me, messenger, I have orders from the general. I am to wake lieutenant Black." said the soldier.

Seizing the opportunity, he said to the soldier, "good luck," and left right away.

The soldier, not understanding Edwin's words, approached the tent and loud snores that could be heard coming from the inside. "Man, even while sleeping he's loud," said the soldier who was sent to get Black. *"Come to think of it, I don't think I've ever seen him more or as quiet as Sirius,"* thought the soldier. Clearing his throat, he entered the tent. "Um, um, lieutenant general sir, general Philip requests your presence at once." There was no response from Black. The soldier tried again, "Um, lieutenant gen..?" He said louder, "Sir Black, sir?" Getting closer he yelled this time, "YOUR PRESENCE IS NEEDED AT ONCE NEXT TO SIR

SMITH." The man was still sound asleep without a care in the world.

"What is all this ruckus, so early in the morning?" a voice was heard asking.

"For crying out loud, who's the moron disturbing my peace?" asked a second grumpy voice.

Startled and alarmed the soldier turned around eyeing the tent in search of the men that spoke up.

"Down here moron?" said the second man. Down on both sides of Black's bed laid the two men. They were so well blended among all that armor and fur that the soldier failed to notice them.

"Come on John, I know you haven't slept for the past couple days but still, this soldier must have a reason requesting Black's presence. Be a little polite would you." Said the first person.

"Always the polite one, uh Robert? I, freaking, need my sleep. State your business idiot." Ordered Lieutenant General John of the soldier.

Straightening himself scared, he informed both men what he was asked to do.

"I see," replied a somewhat calm yet still annoyed superior. Raising a leg John kicked Black as hard as he could on his side whilst still laying down. "Wake up, loudmouth!" shouted him. "Smith needs your assistance!" Black was as solid as a stone. "Was he drinking last night or something?" as he of the soldier.

"Lieutenant Black hasn't been drinking sir. He's been up awake the last five days, sir, surveying the forest for giants." Informed the soldier.

"Ah, he must have found them quite the challenge if he went that far hunting them down." Said Lieutenant General Robert sitting up to face the soldier. "Well, I guess all go instead. If this continues any longer will have two irritated sleep deprive men fighting in this tent. I should go so they may rest."

"I, I shall inform the general then." Said the soldier.

"No need for that, just go back to your post." Ordered Robert.

"Yes sir." Obeyed the young soldier. But before he could completely turn around, Robert asked him a question, "What time is it by the way?"

"I believe it's somewhere around seven close to eight," answered the soldier as he bowed and left.

"Oh wow, barely a 4-hour rest and I am already being disturbed. Go figure what the rest of the will look like." Grumbled John. "I knew I should have gone in the forest away from prying eyes and loudmouth to sleep." Robert could not blame him, having had to endure the king's relentless and careless thirst for fights and adventures, they and the men with them barely got enough sleep. Always hopping all over the place whenever a creature of the dark forest was spotted. In fact, they barely got to fight themselves. But in the end, King Bervard was still their ruler and they had to intervene whenever circumstances appeared dire.

"We swore an oath, John, remember?" said Robert as he had a rather serious look on his face while he grabbed his weapons. Standing over his companion on the ground he continued, "We lost too many good men back then. That is why we go wherever he goes. His recklessness leaves trails of blood. But strong and kind he is though. We fight for those we lost, and those we do not want to lose. Make sure you are fully rested. If Philip needs two of us in the same place, he must fear something. I'll take first point." Said a stern Robert as he left before John could even acknowledge the remembrance of that oath.

"Yeah ..., I remember. One more thing, your kindness is going to be your undoing one day." Mumbled John to himself at Robert who was far gone. Sitting slightly up, he turned to look at Black sound asleep on the bed. "so, the situation was that dire that you took it upon yourself to protect your men huh? Five days? That is a record, even for you. I am sorry for your loss." Offering a somewhat remorseful John as he recalls his rudeness.

"Thanks," was the one word of appreciation that was heard coming from a sleeping Black. Smiling slightly John went back to sleep.

Having already been in full armor, Robert was on his way to Smith. "Smith? Oh no, I forgot to ask the messenger for directions." Scratching his head, he addressed the nearest soldier, "where can I find Lieutenant Smith?"

"Oh, morning Lieutenant Robert. Already rested I see," said the cheerful soldier. "I think he might still be resting sir."

"No, he's awake, he's keeping an eye on the beast." Informed Robert to the soldier.

"Ah, in that case, Lieutenant Smith is somewhere in the forest. Head straight toward the middle of camp then, take a right toward the tree lines. Keep going until you see a downslope within the forest. While you are at the top of the hill, you should see the men below guarding the beast." Informed the soldier.

"Thank you very much, dear sir," said Robert with a slight bow of the head in sign of gratitude. Heading down what was now the main path that separated the left side and right side of camp, he made his way toward the center. *"Huh, he addressed me casually as a lieutenant. Must be Smith's handy work."* though Robert to himself as he walked. "Let's see, that should be about correct. Now a right I take from here," Robert was speaking to himself.

But before he could take that right, his stomach growled just the moment his nose smelled a delicacy of a boar being roasted. "Boar, my favorite! And with just about the right seasoning!" exclaimed the lieutenant. Looking around, he tried to scout which of the men were roasting such savory treats so early in the morning. Following the strong power of his nose, he spotted the culprits. A group of soldiers was gathered in a circle as one of them was slowly turning the boar over a warm fire. *"Yum!"* thought he.

Approaching the men, he cleared his throat, "how much for the whole thing?" he demanded.

"How much?" interject the men roasting the boar, while the men surrounding him turned around to see a lieutenant behind them. Startled, they immediately formally greeted Robert, "good morning Lieutenant Robert, sir!"

Ignoring the men, Robert was fixated on the juicy boar. "How much?" he repeated himself.

"Seriously, you would think that lowly of me, lieutenant?" said the soldier who stayed sitting even though the others stood to greet the lieutenant. "I mean come on Robert, I knew you didn't think much of me, but to think I'd just hand over my food cause you're willing to pay?" continued the man. His casualness was making his companion uneasy, though Robert was known for his kindness, he was also known for his impatience.

Signaling the soldier to move so he could get a good look at the man who was brave enough to speak to him in such a manner, he squinted his eyes at him. The man, at this point still refused to look at Robert. "We shall have a duel then," offered Robert to the man.

"Seriously Robert? How many times do I have to tell you of the authority you hold as a lieutenant? What am I to you? I am certainly not of your rank, so what don't you force me to give it to you?" Dared the man.

"That would be unfair and an abuse of power," returned Robert.

"Urgh, I give up you're a hopeless case." Said the man. Now the other soldiers who were still at this point standing as straight as a needle, in fear of their life for their comrade lack of respect, started to creepily sidestep away from the lieutenant and the cook. Neither the lieutenant nor the man roasting the boar noticed when they disappeared out of sight.

"Hey captain," said a grinning Robert. "Still up to your boasting tactics I see. What are you going to tell your men this time?"

"I'll tell them I sweet-talked you into not punishing me." Laugh the jolly captain.

"Good to see you again Malvin!" greeted Robert.

"And I, you Robert!" returned Malvin. "Glad to see you're in good shape. Am I to assume that these past months have been easy on you?" asked Malvin.

"It had its moments. The king mostly did the fighting, you know how he is, always wanting to test his skills against new beasts and threats. Other than the constant traveling and this sore body, I am well." Replied Robert.

"Good, glad to hear. I saw when you entered the camp, so I convinced the men that you saw with me, to go hunting early in the morning. I knew you would appreciate this juicy grilled boar. Consider it a welcome gift from me to you. A gift among friends. And besides, I doubt you have had yourself a decent meal, since those monsters chased every game in the region farther."

"You sneaky fox. What didn't you just tell me it was for me in the first place?" asked Robert.

"No way, that would ruin my reputation as the disrespectful captain. And besides, I am doing you the biggest favor!" said Malvin.

"Oh yeah, what's that?" asked Robert.

"I am making sure the men fear you as a lieutenant and don't take advantage of your kindness. Somebody has too." Said Malvin as he raised both shoulders in the air.

"What are you going to tell them?" asked Robert.

"Let's see... I'll tell them you promised to report me to the general and see to it that I'm stripped of my title as captain with the possibility of jail time. But that I convinced you not too in exchange that I roast 3 more boars the same as today for you. What do you think? I got my popularity to boost also." Grinned Malvin.

"Sounds like a compromise I would make, except for the punishment part. That's a bit rough, don't you think?" asked Robert.

"Pfff, that's nothing compared to what Lieutenant John would do. Consider myself lucky that I went easy on myself." Said Malvin as both he and Robert burst out laughing. Embracing each other in their arms, they placed a hand on each other's shoulders.

"Thanks!" said an appreciative lieutenant of his captain.

"Come on just say it. You know you want to say it!" teased Malvin.

"Say what? I have nothing else to say."

Clearing his throat, Malvin mimicked his lieutenant's voice, "Thank you so much, Malvin. You are like the brother I never had. However, would I have survived as lieutenant without you? My whole regiment would have taken advantage of me, and I would be leading the weakest of the regiment." Laughed Malvin as Robert had both hands on his hips, a smile on his face, as he listened to his friend monologue what he was thinking. "Was that accurate?" asked Malvin.

"Just about, I'd say." Laughed Robert.

"Good! Now about that boar. You're not leaving here until you've had something to eat." Ordered Malvin

"I can't I have to go. Smith is waiting for me. Well, not me, but I'm a replacement." Informed Robert to his captain.

"You see what I mean, you're too soft. Smith can sit his behind on a rock somewhere. You are not starting today on an empty stomach. I do not care if the other Lieutenant or even the captain and king does it, you are not doing it. I promised your wife I had made sure you eat in the mornings. So, I intend to keep that promise even if I am three months late. Still your fault by the way." Malvin pointed a finger at Robert. "Had you allowed the other lieutenants to give one of their captains to Philip, I'd still be by your side." Complained Malvin.

Having taken a seat at his captain's order, he locked his hands together as he listened to his man. Putting his head down, in a sign of remorse, he knew his captain was right. *"But"* he told himself, *"We can't all be selfish. Somebody has to set an example."* And as if Malvin read his mind, the captain then said, "you can't always be trying to set an example when everybody else already knows what to do, but refuses to, because they know you'll be the first to volunteer. It just doesn't work out that way." Placing a hand on his lieutenant shoulder, lightly yet firmly pressing it, he said as Robert looked him in the eye, "That's why I am your older brother. I have to look out for you. Now I am going to see where I can find you some bread. I saw the baker making some last night, hopefully he still has some stashed away somewhere. You are forbidden to get up from this chair until I permit you. Is that clear?" ordered Malvin of his lieutenant.

"Yes sir." Replied Robert as he held back tears. Of all those Robert had ever done a good deed to, Malvin was the most grateful. Heck, he was the only one who did not try to profit from his kindness.

About three years ago, Malvin's village was invaded by a band of thieves from the kingdom of Serdio. Robert's regiment was in charge of guarding the border. Being as soft as he was, his men got away with about anything. The night the thieves crossed the border into Henri, the guards were drunk as sailors. Making their way inland they plundered and killed and left in their tracks two burned villages, and multiple dead. Sirius was the one who tracked them down for Robert. They found them in the mountains where they had taken prisoners to guide them throughout the land. Malvin and his parents were among them.

Not wanting to risk the lives of citizens, they stayed hidden in the forest looking for a perfect opportunity to attack. That opportunity came when Malvin grabbed one of the thieves' knives and held it at the intruder's throat, threatening to kill his captor if they, the bandits, did not let them go. "You're going to do what if we refuse?" Robert recalled one of them had said. Malvin's parents were trying to reason him to run away instead, for they, just like the rest of the captives, were not as keen-witted to untie themselves as he had done. But it was too late. Two of the bandits walked over to his parents, taking out their swords they forced them in their chest slowly, inflicting great pain and damage. Just like that, they were dead. Had he decided to attack as Sirius had suggested, Malvin's parents would still be alive today.

When everything was settled and the prisoners freed, only the leader of the bandits was left alive. Having still in his hands the knife he had earlier, Malvin was out for vengeance. You could not distinguish if his eyes were full of hatred, anger, or both. But one thing was certain, he had the eyes of an assassin. His parents were everything. And without them, his life no longer mattered. It was now, kill and wait for death. None of the soldiers present had any will to stop Malvin from sheathing blood. None except Robert. He stopped Malvin and told him, "Let me do it. This is too great of a task for you. Your life will not be that of senseless bloodshed."

It was, he Robert, who took the knife from Malvin's hand and dragged the leader of the bandits into the woods. It was he who tortured him for hours, till all was quiet and the sound of forest life could be heard again. None dared stopped Robert that day. All were shocked at this kind man's new nature. None ever saw what Robert looked like during that time except for Malvin who had followed him, without his knowing. "Teach me," was all he asked of Robert, as Robert wiped the blood off his hands when the screams of torture were no more.

Later Robert found out that Malvin was sixteen, old enough to join the ranks. He eventually agreed to take the lad and trained him himself. Passing every training and excelling in combat, Robert pulled a few strings to have the young

Malvin as captain of his regiment. The youngest captain in history. It was, he, Malvin that brought back order into the regiment. He challenged every captain in Robert's regiment to a near-death duel. And without mercy, he humiliated every last one of them. So much so that he requested that all those who lost against him be removed as captain and made to join the ranks like regular soldiers. His arguments back then were the fact that they failed to guard the border and keep their men in line. An argument that everyone besides the disorganized regiment agreed with.

And that was the reason why he, Robert, sent him with Philip. The kid had many enemies, and not knowing with whom he would have his back against, Robert did not want for his men, precisely the ex-captains, to stab him in the back and blame it on battle wounds. He was always looking out for him. Malvin is the reason why he swore not to give in to the evil he keeps locks away inside of him, ever again.

CHAPTER 6

Brothers

Heading toward the king's tent, Philip was determined to make sure nothing happened to his brother. If he died, the queen would never forgive him. Not only was it his duty as general but more so as the king's brother.

Arriving at the entrance of the royal tent, he burst in so fast that the guards posted at the entrance did not have time to greet him. "Bervard, we need to talk immediately." Said Philip to a snoring king. The king was dead asleep. His body laid lifeless on the bed. The only apparent sign that he was alive, aside from his snore, was the rising and falling of his chest. "For God's sake Bervard get up would you," ordered Philip to his younger brother. Feeling a bit irritated due to the urgency of the matter, he grabs Bervard by the shoulders and shook him awake.

Bervard being a king and a warrior did not take it too well. The first thing he did as he opened his eyes was to grab his sword that laid on the bed on his right; and in a slashing motion from right to left he took aim for the intruder's throat. Philip being quick, pulled his sword from its sheath, on his left side, and blocked the king's blade. "Good to see you're awake now. What would have happened, if I may ask, had I not been armed?" asked Philip of his brother.

Surprised that Philip stood before him, Bervard cleared his vision. Philip continued the questioning, "Let's say we were under attack and I sent someone to wake you up and get you to safety?" Sitting up, Bervard straightened his composure and answered in a straight face, "I guess you would both be dead."

"When human life should be protected, you lack in your duty to protect it. You charge in needlessly and don't think about anything else but your enjoyment in battle. You don't think of the consequences and that's my problem with you." Criticized Philip. "Think before you act, it would help us out a lot."

This was the relationship between the two. Philip was the oldest brother. He gave up the throne for the sake of Henri's protection. He knew that Bervard would be in no shape to defend it in times of war. A great fighter was he. He could take down any foe and or beast. But when it came to strategy and keeping losses to a minimum, he was no good at that. Unable is he to think on the eve of battle or during battle. And that is what Philip held against his brother. Since at a young age, Bervard used to get in trouble, and Philip had to get him out. And when they were old enough to hold a sword, Bervard always searched for something or someone greater than himself to challenge. May it be a wild bear or even a giant snake, he never backed down from a fight. And that's where the problem laid.

Being a prince and now king, it was the soldiers' prime duty was to safeguard the crown. If anything happened to the king, they would be held responsible. This is why in his attempt to capture wild beasts many soldiers got hurt in the process. Instead of strategizing and using his men effectively, he kept them at bay. But that was also the reason why his subjects liked him. He was fierce. When a beast from the mountains came down and wreaked havoc in the villages, the king waited for no one. He charges in and fought it till the beast was slain and the head brought back to the capital for all to see his glory. I guess you could say that's why the soldiers admire him, despite that being for Philip recklessness. Philip did not like the funerals.

Taking a deep breath, he sighed, "look, I think you may be in danger." Informed Philip. "But first tell me about your travels. What sorts of creatures did you face off against these four months?" asked Philip.

Motioning toward a jar of water nearby, Philip poured some in a cup for his brother and handed it to him. Swallowing it in one go, he got up from his bed and sat on a nearby stool. Glancing at his sword on the bed then back a Philip, he said "Sorry about that. I hadn't been able to rest up until now. I had to stretch my numbers in-between villages." Said Bervard.

"Why didn't you send for more men?" asked Philip.

"The men refused. They wanted to do this themselves. They wanted to prove their worth." Said Bervard.

"And lose life in the process no doubt." Returned Bervard sharply.

"You're wrong." Said Bervard in a strong tone of voice. "I lost no men, nor villagers, save that which died before we got there. The men are more capable than you think, you know. You should stop trying to protect them and let them thrill at the battle. Greater is the glory for the men who dies knowing he dies for a great cause."

This was where they butted heads. Where they refused to see eye to eye. Philip was a strategist, Bervard was the fearless conqueror.

"Anyhow," Bervard continued, "What we faced were mostly critters, that's what I call them anyway. They mostly stayed hidden in fields of tall grass and crops and attacked at night. They were of no real harm alone. But in a group, they could take you down and kill you with their claws, or nails, or whatever they are. They were the most numerous. We would free one village and leave for the next, only to later realize they were back."

"What? They came back alive?" asked Philip.

"No, they didn't. We burned what we killed. There were just that many. Towards the end, when we managed to corner them in a wheat field, I ordered it to set it ablaze. So, that is one village that will need our assistance this coming winter. Anyhow, have you seen where the guards put my boxes?"

"Your boxes? What's in them?" asked Philip.

"The spoils of war," answered a smiling king. "Give me a moment, I think you'd better be able to imagine the troublesome creatures if you saw one." Grinned Bervard.

"Don't tell me you kept one alive?" said Philip in an almost shocked voice.

"It was alive, but it died. Most likely due to starvation." Said Bervard as he exited his tent. "Wait here...," he started to say, "on second thought come with me." Walking side by side they headed out toward the king's wagon. Upon nearing it, the first thing that caught Philip's attention was the stench.

"Good grieve, what is that smell?!" Exclaimed Philip as he raised his forearm to his nose.

"That brother is the smell of four months of victory. A villager gave us this wagon as a sign of gratitude. So, it made carrying the trophies so much easier." Smiled the king as he looked back at the wagon.

"And how many trophies do you need?" asked Philip as he found a wagon full of boxes to be outrageous.

"I just need three. One for each creature we faced." Replied the king, smiling knowing full well what Philip was going to say next.

"And yet there are twenty-something boxes on there."

"Oh yeah," started the king as if he forgot that fact. Grinning he replied to Philip. "Since the wagon came in handy, some of the men with me, wanted to take for themselves memories of their victory."

"Who under this heaven would dare skin them for you I wonder? The smell is awful. I hope you're not thinking of going to the castle with that death smelling wagon." Warned Philip.

"Fine, my men and I will skin it ourselves. How hard could it be?" Laughed Bervard. "Anyhow," getting on the wagon, Bervard opened one of the stocked boxes, "come on up, I want to show you what they look like."

Philip thought the smell could not have gotten any worse. He was wrong. The freshly open box contaminated the air around them. So much so that he thought he was going to vomit. "Come on, hurry up, that's an order." Ordered Bervard of Philip to come and see. Reluctantly and holding his breath, Philip joined his brother on the wagon.

"Oh God!" said Philip before he vomited inside the open box.

Standing next to him was a laughing king who seemed satisfied at the side effect the smell caused his brother. "I won the bet!" yelled the king.

"What are you blabbering about?" asked Philip as he tried to control himself from vomiting further. Regaining his composure, he turned toward a king whose hands were on his hips as he glanced out toward camp. Looking at what Bervard was glancing at, he caught sight of a soldier going about collecting money from others. They were being watched this whole time and he failed to notice it. "Are you serious? Did you really gamble my health away?" asked Philip.

"Yep, and I'm getting quite the sum for it too." Smirked Bervard. "I had two-hundred and fifty men with me. Half of them placed bets against you. I'll let you do the math, at five silver coins each." Said the king as he was satisfied with his investment.

"I can't believe you. So, this one box is the rotten one huh?"

"If only you had realized that sooner, I'd have lost that bet. Too bad!" said Bervard as he leaned down to weigh the bags of silver from the collector soldier. "That's quite the sum we have there." Said Bervard. "Where's the nearest village?" asked the king of Philip and the soldier.

"About an hour west. Why?" asked Philip.

"Good. Take one of Philip's carts, take ten men with you, go to that village, and bring back Ales' worth for the whole lot of us. Protect the ale as you would protect me. Got that soldier?" Ordered the king to the cheery soldier.

"Yes, my King!" exclaimed the happy soldier. He was gone the moment he was done taking orders.

"I'd say they'll be back in an hour and a half top. What do you think?" asked Bervard of Philip.

"I give up." Said a defeated Philip. "I'm doom to watch over you till I die." At that, they both laughed.

Waving to nearby soldiers, the king ordered that the decomposed crate of the creature be burned. Taking down the crate, the soldiers themselves were having a hard time breathing, but they managed to carry it away without vomiting. Going back to the task at hand, the king opened a different crate. This time revealing the remains of a hideous creature. "Woah," was all Philip could say. "That's nothing, you should have seen the trouble we had hunting them in high grass," responded Bervard. The dead creature that laid in the crates had very thin arms and legs that could bend the same way as a four-legged animal. The palm of its hands was no different from its arms and legs in size. Very thin and small palm which contained at its extremity long fingers and claws. Its small feet contained razor-sharp and pointy nails.

With a disproportionate lower body to that of its upper body, its size and weightlessness allowed for it to maneuver at fast speed. With a hole on both sides of its head surrounded by a bunch of wrinkled up skin formed its triangular head. A bald scalp, that perhaps was slimy when alive. It was of a dirty beige color.

"Those nails you see there could tear through armor. Just imagine what it'll do to your skin." Said Bervard.

"Small yet dangerous. Easy to underestimate." Replied Philip. "I'm thinking this is more than just some random attack or escape."

"Like someone sent them to scout ahead I presume you're going to tell me?" Said Bervard.

"Exactly." acknowledge Philip.

"Yeah, I was getting the same impression as we were hunting them down." Said Bervard. "But it doesn't matter what came out or will come out of that forest, I'll kill them all."

"If history is correct, we'll need more than just you to fight off the evil that thrones in the dark forest. If these things can shred armor, imagine what more hideous creatures' lies within, waiting to get out." Said Philip.

"If he, she, it, is still alive that is. Who knows, maybe history is wrong. Maybe whoever it is, is now dead or weak, and so the barrier is failing because of that. Please, you would really believe dragons gave humans powers to become living barrier lock keepers. We are humans, they are dragons. We're food in their eyes!" revolted the King at the knowledge that humans would need the help of extinct dragons.

"Your cynicism and disbelief may get you killed one day." Retorted Philip. It was no use even talking to him at this point. "He'd want to stay and face whatever else lurks in these woods," thought Philip. Hoping off the wagon, he tried to control his emotions. Though tension between Henri and Serdio was high at the borders, Philip and the queen of Serdio were in good relations. In fact, it was she, the queen of Serdio, that had summoned Philip to inform him of the origin of the children of darkness that laid in waiting in that treacherous forest. A summoned in the disguise of peace talks. She feared, she would later reveal to Philip that her husband did not take her nor the existential threat seriously.

For generations, her bloodline had passed down the history of what was. She was royalty, her husband was not, thus why his disbelief. But as the years went by, she watched as her kingdom fell to lawlessness. And the king, her foolish husband, given leeway to his soldiers to do as they please. A sign she saw was the fall of Serdio. So, to ensure that the knowledge of history was kept alive she prepared peace talks with the kingdom of Henri. Peace talks which would never have had to take place, had her subjects respected themselves and did not every now and then invade Henri.

Knowing who the king was and how he, like her husband were foolish, act first, think never fools, she specifically asked for Philip. "Since I will be leading the peace talks, it is unnecessary for your majesty to attend. If we can come to an agreement, then shall both kings meet to discuss further matters, and thus why the presence of your general shall do," had she written in her letter to the royal of Henri. Philip at first did not believe her of course. That is until the queen had done a terrible thing that went against her status. It was not so much as to what Philip saw, but what he witnessed her do; had her kingdom known of this she would be considered a traitor and even accused of indecency.

Philip being the cautious man that he always is, was not buying a single word she was saying. In his mind, "she brought me this close to her borders to have me assassinated. Me dead, and the kingdom's defense falls in ruins." At least now he knows that was not the case, and that though relations sour between the two nations, it was no fault of the queen, but of the men in ruling seats. Indifferent to do anything about it while a common enemy lying in the shadows for centuries awaits a rebirth.

Having called Philip to her tent, and Philip accepting the invitation on the agreement that his men surround the tent and area with no trace of her soldiers to be found. *"You'll never agree to that,"* had thought he back then. But to his surprise she had. They, Philip and the queen, queen Erlen, were alone in the tent. She was alone with him surrounded by her enemies. "I understand why you doubt. I would myself. But the facts are there. What I am about to show you will prove true what I have told you. Once that's done, you must inform your majesties of everything I have said." Had said queen Erlen.

Turning her back to Philip, she began to undress. "Forgive my indecency, but this the best way I can convince you. And if you fear that I shall accuse you of having tried to force yourself unto me, then my life you may freely take."

Harsh and shocking words for a queen. Putting a hand on his sword to hammer down a critical blow if she indeed had such thoughts. He cares more about his honor than being afraid of a full-fledged war. "Remember what I told you about the seals," said queen Erlen as she was done undoing the button on her corset. Dropping the top half of her dress to her waists, her naked back revealed a circular golden flame seal. The seal was alive, faintly changing in intensity. From dark golden flames colors to light golden ones. Indeed, had it been of a solid color, Philip would have considered it nothing more but body paint.

Philip was stupefied. "You must come with me. You must show this to king Bervard and Queen Miriam. They'll most likely believe and be willing to act if they see it themselves." Had said Philip back then.

"How much lower must I humiliate myself before you and your people? My current humiliation, isn't it enough to take with you and have them believe? If what I have just done is find out of my people, it will be enough for war and my beheading. Therefore, I ask this of you, Sir Philip," said the queen as she clothed her back, "you can tell your majesties everything that I have told you, but mention nothing of how I convinced you. I can live with my humiliation, but the gossip that would arise afterward would kill me."

"You ask a lot of me, your highness. Without that seal, they will most likely be skeptical. But skepticism is better than disbelief I suppose." Said Philip as queen Erlen, having fixed herself turned to face him. Taking a knee to the floor, Philip bowed before queen Erlen. "If you must throw your honor away before me for the sake of our survival, then I shall do the same. GUARDS!" yelled Philip at his men that surrounded the tent and forest. Immediately the captain of the royal guards along with his men, burst through the tent sword in hand ready to strike, only to find a frightened queen and the general on his knees.

"What is the meaning of this?" had asked the captain of Philip.

Without getting up, with his knees still against the floor, he turned to the captain. "Queen Erlen has dismayed her status as a royal, not for peace talks," said Philip turning to Erlen to only find her with frightened and teary eyes. She was holding her breath for what Philip was going to say next. It was either going to help her cause or kill her where she stood. Philip continued, "I'm afraid, but for a matter of uttermost importance that threatens our mutual survival."

"And that's to explain why you're kneeling before a queen that isn't your own? Did she bewitch you or something?" Said an angry captain as he advanced intending to strike the queen if that were the case.

"Stand down, Irwin. She's not the enemy." Said Philip. Looking at the other men in the tent, he ordered, "Take down the tent." Without hesitating, the guards executed their orders. Through it all, Philip did not once get up, he stayed on his knee for all his men to see. And when the tent was out of the way, and they were visible to all, Philip spoke up. "Men, do not feel indignant that I bow before a queen that is not my own. I shall explain what happened." At these words, Queen Erlen could no longer hold back her tears. They ran down her cheeks the same way rain droplets fell on a window. Where one drop of rain lands on a window or surface, it glides down the surface making a way for all the incoming droplets to follow in its trace. Thus, were her tears.

"Queen Erlen did not want to meet me here for peace talks but rather for matters of utmost urgency that should cause us to lay aside our petty feud." Continued Philip.

"What about our men that died, you call their death and memory petty too?" came an angry response from among Philips men, followed by other soldiers joining in their voices too.

"LISTEN TO YOUR GENERAL!" Philip yelled. He felt the urge to get up and bring his men back to order. Of course, what could they understand? They did not see what he saw. "The next person to interrupt me shall be made an example of." Warned Philip. "The reason why I bow is because of what is about to happen to her majesty. She will be looked down upon, for thinking she could call our nations to make peace. She will be made fun of by her people and ours and certainly most importantly by her king." Said Philip, to which the soldiers laughed. They, the soldiers, now started to think that Philip was making fun of her by bowing.

With a stern yet concerned look on his face, Philip looked at his men, then at the queen. It was a hopeless case trying to explain it to them. What he wanted to do, was show his gratitude toward queen Erlen for her courage and humility. This was his way of humiliating himself before her and to level the humiliation, he wanted his men to do the same. Dropping his head down, he whispered, "It's hopeless," to which Irwin, who stood behind him heard.

"General, answer me this. Are you making fun of her or are you serious?" asked Irwin.

"I am dead serious. I wouldn't do this as a joke." Answered Philip.

Looking into the eyes of his general and knowing who he was, Irwin decided to believe him. Putting away his sword, Irwin advanced beside Philip, and ordered the men, to bow before queen Erlen. Being known for his ruthlessness he barked threats at those who would not do as he said. Threats they knew, he always fulfilled. Leading by example, he bowed a knee before the queen of Serdio, followed by a shuffling of the armor of the soldiers of Henri doing the same. Seeing what unfolded before her, Erlen could no longer hold back her rivers of tears, nor could she hold back her sobering voice.

Getting back up and ordering everyone else to do the same, Philip asked that the tent be set up again. Ordering everyone out, Philip stayed alone with the queen.

"Had I come to you the day I became queen; I would not have had to carry this burden alone. Enduring my husband's mockery would have not been as painful as it is now." Said Erlen.

"If you had come to me early, you would not probably have gotten the same result that you got today. History and events are things we wish we could change. But how things happen must sometimes be accepted without wishing for a different outcome. Things happen when they should, and little control we have over them." Replied Philip.

Bowing his head before Erlen, Philip turned around to leave. "Wait," called out Erlen. "The seal that you have seen," started Erlen.

"Don't worry, I shall not mention how you showed me," reassured Philip.

"Thank you. But that's not it. What I am about to tell must be kept to yourself. In no way should people find out about it. My husband doesn't," she paused at what she wanted to say. "Few believe me about what I've told you. Therefore, this I have hidden from everyone. I entrust that it can help you in the future. When I give birth," Erlen started to say but to Philip's dismay, he was puzzled as to what giving birth had to do with this. *"Is she pregnant and hid that fact from her husband? I hope she's not going to ask me to take care of her child."* Conversed Philip in his head.

"When I give birth, the seal on my back will slowly fade and will be passed down to my firstborn, regardless if it's a girl or boy. And when I die, the seal will have been completely transferred." Revealed Queen Erlen.

"Why are you telling me this?" asked Philip. "Wait, when you die? What happens if you die now?"

"If I were to die, without an heir to inherit it, then what lies in waiting in the dark forest will be one step closer to freedom. And even if I do give birth, it will take a full twenty years for it to be passed down. And on my deathbed, the transfer will be complete. Meaning if I died in between the twenty years, a half seal or however amount is transferred over, is nothing more than a twig before a horse." Revealed Erlen.

Philip did not just hear her words, but he also heard what she was not saying. *"Your kingdom is in ruin and falling apart, is that it?"* He questioned himself.

CHAPTER 7

Tish - Darker than Coal

Philip having been lost in the memories of the past and why he among everyone else took the threat seriously, became conscious that he had stopped walking. Looking up at his surroundings, he found the majority of the soldiers were looking at him. Turning around, he could still see his brother was still on the wagon, hands on his hips with a puzzled look on his face. Looking down for words to say, Philip raised his head and said, "If you insist on fighting it, then it'll be after you fully rest. Meaning, not today but tomorrow. Understood?" demanded Philip.

"Aye!" said the king, knowing that Philip would not restrict his desire to fight.

Letting go of his anger, Philip continued walking but without a real destination. As he walked past the rows of tents that the soldiers had set up for themselves, he heard a familiar voice. Focusing on the source and location, he found that the familiar voice was hiding behind a tent on the far-left sideline of camp. And hiding alone, it was not. There before it, the familiar voice was a roasting boar. A deliciously smelling boar, with a younger man slowly turning it over a fire. Advancing into view, Philip found that Robert was the familiar voice. "I figured it would be you." Said Philip. "What are you doing here? Aren't you supposed to be resting?"

"Morning General! I got enough rest for now. I am actually on my way to Smith but this juicy tender delicious boar you see here caught my attention." Revealed Robert.

"The smell enough proves your innocence." Admitted Philip as he looked at the young man. "I know you." Said he to the man.

"Aye, indeed you do. Malvin, would you please stand so Philip can see how much you've grown." Asked Robert.

Getting up and somewhat uneasy that Robert called Philip without his proper title in his presence he greeted the general, "good morning general."

Eyeing Malvin, Philip recounted the events that led to Robert taking him in as son and brother and in the end, training him as a knight. Impressed by the young man's status and looks, Philip said, "I'd say, Robert, if you wanted to retire, you can do it now. I've just found your replacement."

"And I'd want none other." Affirmed Robert.

Giving Robert a concerned look, Malvin asked, "retirement?"

"I'm thinking about it. I am getting old and nearing fifty-five. I'm not as able as I used to, well not that I am incapable, but you'll be perfect to take my place." Revealed Robert.

"No, you can't. If you leave, I leave. I do not want to be given the status of lieutenant I want to earn it. I want to climb the ranks. If I replace you now, the men will never really respect me nor follow me." Complained Malvin.

"The kid is dedicated. I approve of your choice." Said Philip as he turned to leave but doing the opposite immediately. Pulling out his knife, he advanced toward the fire and carved himself a couple of boar ribs. Putting it to his mouth, he savored it as if it was his first delicious treat. "Amazing! Robert, shame on you for not knowing how to cook. Shame on you for not telling me how amazing a cook he is. I would have done as if I were in the castle." Reproached a humorous Philip. "Anyhow, don't stay too long, you don't want to keep Smith waiting. No, no sit, sit." Waved him to Robert who was about to get up. "I'm going to him now. I will tell him you are coming. Just bring him some meat, I'm sure he'll appreciate it." Said he as he turned and left.

Unbeknownst to Malvin, and Robert, the soldiers that were previously there, before Robert came and interrupted them, were not far off. They were waiting for Robert to leave to have their turn at eating. "Damn, first lieutenant Robert, now the general, if the king and lieutenant John finds out, there will be nothing left." Whispered a teary-eyed soldier.

Nearing Smith and with a satisfied belly, Philip tried to sneak up behind him. Pulling out his knife, he advanced toward his target. Having waved to the soldiers around to not look his way, he continued his sneak attack without interruptions. Taking the opportunity of Smith dropping his guard while he stretched, Philip tapped the knife against Smith's right side and said, "You're getting old Smith, you let your guard down."

Smith having sensed the intruder, and seeing how at that moment, the soldiers across from him and to his sides were trying hard to avoid looking his way, he figured someone was behind him. And that someone had to be someone in authority to try and sneak upon him. Stretching his arms upwards, he purposely created an opening for whoever was behind him. With the intruder busy savoring that opening, Smith, with his arms still outstretched upwards, reached into his sleeves and pulled out a dagger. Tapping Philip on the back of the neck with, he said, "I don't think so."

Surprised, Philip walked around Smith and stood in front of him. Looking at each other, they laugh as they both put their weapon back in their spot. "You went too fast for that opening General." Said Smith.

"Aye, looks like I'm the one getting rusty." Agreed Philip.

"How did it go with the king?" asked Smith

"Stubborn as ever." Reply Philip.

"No surprise there. So, why are you back here then?" asked Smith of his general.

"Honestly," Philip paused, "I don't know. I stopped on the way and found Robert. By the way, Robert is coming, not Black. He's coming with breakfast too, thus why he's taking a while to come."

"Well, if it's for me, I guess I can overlook his lateness," joked Smith as he could tell Philip was lost in thoughts. "Well then general, it'll be best for you to rest up then uh. I can take it from here."

"Thank you, Smith." Thanked Philip, without uttering another word he departed for some much overdue rest.

By now, the fast runner was settling down. It was no longer as agitated to escape as in the previous days. *"No doubt from tiredness,"* thought Smith. When fully stretched and not crouching for attacks, it looked about twice the size of a mountain lion. *"Fast, dangerous, and big, no wonder we lost men,"* Smith acknowledged. With giant claws and sharp long teeth, of the creatures they have had to fight, it seems the most normal looking. Smith hated to imagine what else was given birth and breathes inside the dark forest.

The peculiar thing about the creature was the fact that it was very observant and somewhat intelligent. Smith and Philip made notice of this when they were in its presence. It would stare at them almost as if trying to make sense of what they were saying. And when soldiers came to take post, its expression was of that of studying them. As if committing to memory everything and everyone that came into view. Smith now understood and agreed with Philip being concerned for the king's safety. Wasting no time, he ordered the soldiers to shoot more arrows into the beast, who barely reacted to any signs of pain. Anchoring the beast down, Smith was taking no chances.

Sitting down and resting his back against a tree, Smith laid his spear on the ground. Taking out a piece of parchment and charcoal, he jotted away. When he was done writing he handed it over to one of the soldiers near him and asked that it be given to Lieutenant John without delay. Bringing his legs closer under his belly and crossing them, he took his spear and planted the tip in the ground. Smith did this for one reason only. Being on the floor, if ever the need came for him to get up quickly, he would only need to use his spear as support to get off the floor and be able to also use it in a defensive offensive stance.

Not far off, from his sitting position, on his left from behind the beast, Smith could see Robert coming downhill to meet him. In his hand, he had two large plates of food and a jar of ale.

"Hey, Smith!" greeted Robert as he got close to his comrade.

"Robert." Smith returned the greeting. "Took you long enough to get here. If I am correct, you took about an hour and a half."

"Well, I would have gotten here sooner, but my nose caught wind of this delicious meat you see before you. And believe me, I know the cook, so this was, is, definitely worth it. And besides, had I gotten here any sooner, we would have missed out on this ale." Explained Robert as he lifted the jug.

"Who ordered that?" asked Smith.

"The king won a bet against Philip and had men buy it for the camp." Informed Robert

"I doubt it'll last us through mid-day." Joked Smith. "Anyhow if one those pates are for me, then I'll gladly overlook your lateness and try not to embarrass you in front of your men." Said Smith.

"Ah, ah, ah," laugh Robert sarcastically. "As if you could." Said he as he handed Smith one of the plates he had in hand and down sat next to him.

"Oh, you still don't believe me capable of beating you in a duel uh?" asked Smith.

"I know so. We have had that conversation before and yeah, that is not happening. The only one who can beat me in a duel is Sirius and Irwin. Maybe Philip, but I doubt that." Said a reflective Robert.

"Irwin, I know he can beat you. Sirius? I think you let him win on purpose. He is the best tracker among us. The best spy. He has no equal when it comes to espionage but fighting heck all four of us beat him. Except you, why is that?" asked Smith.

"I see. So, none of you have yet to figure him out. He lets you guys win on purpose. Why? I do not know. But when we duel, he does not hold back. Ever. So, to say, all four of you can beat him and I cannot, would mean that I am weaker than him. And that is far from the truth." Argued Robert.

"There's one way to settle this, a duel." Said an excited Smith.

"You're on. Choose the time, place, and weapon. You will be no match for me. Bet what you want carefully because you will lose it." Returned Robert as he foresaw the outcome of the duel.

Smith and Robert were good friends and even closer as comrades. They loved to disagree and argue. This was nothing new to them. Whenever they had a difference in opinion, they would try to solve it in a manner that brought excitement, and today was no different.

"This shall be our first official duel outside of training, will it not?" asked Smith.

"Indeed, and believe me, you're going to regret this." Grinned Robert as they both stopped talking and began to eat.

"I always wondered why you go easy on the others and not on me. Was it? Is it because of that day? Did you, just as Malvin see me in my rage? If that is the case, what exactly are you trying to do? Why push me to the extreme? Are we the same, you and me? If not in personality, then in skills maybe? No matter your reasons, if you don't hold back for me, then I'll just have to defeat you for you to tell me." Robert was lost in thought. Realizing it, he continued to eat and laid aside he's comrade mysterious ways. "Speaking of Sirius, where is he? I haven't seen him since I got here." Asked Robert of Smith.

"Honestly, I have no idea. I imagine he must have found something interesting to scout, otherwise, he'd be back by now." Answered Smith.

"How long has he been gone?" asked Robert.

"Two days. Have not seen him for two days. He must be following something. In any case, I am sure he will be back to inform us of his finding. He's not the type to ever get lost either." Assured Smith.

Sirius was indeed the best tracker in Henri. He could find anyone or animal. Even someone who did not want to be found. His tracking skills were like an extension of his arms. They were a part of him, and he could not rid himself of the gift. Two days and a half ago, when all was quiet and calm after the battles were fought and one-eyed giants were no more, Sirius noticed, did not see anything, but noticed something peculiar among the branches. Green leaves were falling from the branches above. He only noticed it. The branches being thick at the top of the trees made a perfect spot for a spy. From that height, and within those thick branches, someone or something would be in a perfect position to observe everything happening below. And so, without giving away the fact that he noticed whatever was in the trees, he kept an eye on it.

When it left the forest, Sirius tracked it down without revealing to the perpetrator that he was doing so. Leaving his armor behind, he only had his weapons and cloak. A cloak that was dark black and green on the other. Sirius has been tracking the enemy for three days now. An enemy that was highly intuitive. Different from its kind. It was smart to stay among the treetop and not come down as the others did. It was highly intelligent too, stopping now and then to check and make sure no one was following. Better yet, it was going around in circles trying to lose whoever was following it. And effort it gave up since Sirius never revealed his presence.

It was on that third day, near the border with Serdio that Sirius learned of a bigger plot that would upset the balance of power in both nations. There at the border, the thing that was hopping among the trees made landfall. Sirius still hidden, seeing what he was tracking down, now really had reasons to stay hidden. One false move would mean not just the end, but a cruel torturous one.

There at the border, the beast he was tracking was walking toward Serdians soldiers. Though Sirius could feel fear rising just at the sight of it, the soldiers were not the least bit scared. The beast that was before him, was of the same kind that they killed. One-eyed club-wielding giant. The only difference was that this one was a fur, greyish white and a lot taller than the others. Surprise at the turn of events, Sirius was contemplating going back to warn the King, when the unexpected happened. It talked.

"I lost my brothers. The humans killed them. I saw a human giving the orders. Must have been the one in charge, but not the one we are looking for. He was not wearing a crown. He must be in the fields. We should attack now. They are apart. With them gone, the land will be easy to overtake." Said the beast to the Serdian soldiers.

"Doesn't matter," said the soldier, "the general has changed his plans. More of your kind and others were able to escape the barrier. We no longer need to destroy Henri to overthrow the crown. We have enough numbers now to defend the border as we attack the castle. All who aren't with us will die."

"Leave those who won't join our ranks to us. Just focus on eliminating the crown. For that barrier to fall, we need to get rid of the crown. One of them carries the seal to unlock the barrier. Kill everyone, leave none alive." Said the beast as it turned and headed toward a dark spot in the forest.

"What do they call you?" yelled the soldier to the beast before leaving.

Turning around, the one eye club giant looked at the soldier and said, "We are cyclops."

Continuing its walking halfway toward the shadow, cyclops stopped, as the shadow itself grew and expanded toward it. Sirius was witnessing all this. He did not dare move, did not dare speak. Did not dare breathe. One wrong move could mean the end. He now took to heart the stories of what was within that barrier. Of its origin. But most importantly of what, or rather, who laid at its center. And if the royals of Serdio held the key to keep it locked, then it was time for both kings to set aside their differences.

Sirius watched as the shadow grew and came closer and closer to the cyclops. *"NO! It can't be."* Realize Sirius. The shadow was not growing. It was not expanding. It was in itself alive. What seemed like a shadow was a living beast. It absorbed even the light of the setting sun. Thus, why Sirius first thought it was a shadow. Expanding its wings and walking up to the cyclops, Sirius could decipher its form. It was a dragon. A black dragon.

"Tish." Said the cyclops in a deep voice.

CHAPTER 8

The Objective

"Tish." Called out the cyclops to the dragon as it got closer to him.

"Do they suspect anything?" asked the dragon

"It doesn't seem so. But they aren't scared of us either." Replied the cyclops.

"Then it would seem that they at least believe in our existence." Said Tish.

"There was this human, giving out orders. They called him general. He kept repeating 'this is the day I told you would come. A day when the darkness of the forest comes to hunt us.'" Informed the cyclops to the dragon.

In all this, Sirius did not dare move. He feared being spotted by the dragon that was facing him. The cyclops had its back toward Sirius which was a good thing. Having hidden behind tall bushes, he used his cloak as camouflage to become one with it. No sooner than he had done so, that an enemy approached from behind. An enemy tall enough to walk over both him and the bushes. It was as tall as the cyclops but taller if it could stand straight. With razor-sharp nails and a slimy dirty beige skin, the creature walked past and over him.

"I see you're back. And alone just like me." Said the new creature in an almost shrieking tone of voice. "I knew I should have brought bigger ones of my children. The little ones were of no match for them. At least I know what they are and not capable of. Their armors are no match for our blades." Said the creature as it looked at its nails.

"Did you notice their king among them?" asked the dragon.

"I did. He was the ruthless one among his men. He enjoyed killing my children." Said the long nail creature.

"Do you know where he is now?" asked Tish the dragon.

"No, I lost him in the plains. There was nowhere else to hide to follow them. He did not head back to the castle. So, he must still be somewhere in the land. Why not send more shriekers, more of me to seek him out?" asked the shrieker.

"We can't risk him alarming the whole land before we can fully collapse the barrier. We still have the element of surprise. If we can wipe them all out, then we won't risk messengers seeking fighters from other lands like last time." Said Tish.

"Have none joined our ranks?" asked the Cyclops.

"None." Replied the dragon. "Which is why we had to kill all the outposts along both borders. They are loyal to their king and queen of Serdio, unlike the Serdian general and his soldiers. Those idiots do not know what they have unleashed. They think they will reign once their king is dead. If only they knew. Thanks to their ignorance and service, mother was able to help us escape the barrier. Who knew that those innocent could enter the barrier and yet those full of evil like ourselves cannot enter nor leave.

But with the proper exchange of good going in we were able to escape that prison. And now the others waiting to get out have food in exchange to feast upon. It is perfect. Can you hear them crying for more human blood?" humored the dragon in a cold dark steady voice.

Just then a Serdian soldier approached the three leaders, interrupting their meeting. "Everything has been made ready. Every village has been cut off from each other, so there's no risking a messenger warning the castle."

"Does your king not suspect your general?" asked Cyclops.

"Not at all. His a foolish one." Said the soldier.

"Aren't you all?" Said shrieker with an almost sarcastic tone of voice, that caused Tish to give him a cold warning stare.

The soldier not witted enough to understand that, or rather, just power-hungry for violence, continued, "the king still thinks that we're trying to contain an epidemic. But the queen, she is a different story. She has never let her guards down. It is a good thing one of the villages we pushed through the barrier managed to escape. His body was full of boils. We took it to the queen as proof of the epidemic."

"She believes you then?" asked Tish.

"Barely. Knowing her, she'll probably try and send out spies to check our reports." Revealed the soldier. "No worries, we have as prisoner someone who knows every secret passage to and from the castle. All spies will be intercepted. Why not attack now?" asked the soldier.

"Based on the information your general gave us. There are those among you that holds the keys to the barrier. We cannot risk them escaping otherwise mother will be trapped there forever. You do not have enough innocent humans that can offset the power balance of the barrier to free us all. Which is why we need to find those ten humans. We shall attack together. Simultaneously. Besides, there is no need to rush this since my kind is no more in this land. Correct?" asked Tish.

"That is correct. We have not seen or heard of a dragon sighting in centuries." Assured the soldier.

"Perfect," Tish replied in a slow satisfied speech.

"So, what, even if your kind were still alive, they'd be no match for us. Heck, we can take you on ourselves. Mother's the one who put you in charge of us, don't forget it." Said shrieker in a challenging tone of voice.

"Oh, don't fool yourselves comrades. I lost all interest in battle the day I fought my brother. The only thing I longed for was to face him again. Do not fool yourselves, the dragon you see," Tish's voice grew deeper, "before you, is much, much more capable then the likes of your kinds combine." Said Tish as it stood up fully on all four legs; revealing a height that surpassed both the cyclops and shrieker. "It took seven of my kind to imprison me. Out of the seven, I killed two. And if you think it was a simple battle. You are strongly mistaken." Said it as he looked at the two separately. "The battle raged on for days as the barrier was being created. Days. If you think you can take me on, I'll gladly accept your challenges." Looking at Shrieker it said, "Don't bother thinking your boils effect slime will harm me in any way. My scales are tough enough that not even your blades can pierce. I've long to have a full course meal, and you would do just fine. Just as your little ones when roasted. So, if you both want to break rank and act like those humans," it shouted out in hatred, "then go ahead. I'll gladly feast on your flesh and carry this mission myself."

Sirius could see a concerned look on the soldier's face. A face that started to question the integrity of their actions. Of what they have done and about to do. A face that believed every word Tish said. One that revealed that, if this dragon decided to go, rogue, there would be nothing to stop it. The Cyclops understanding this spoke up, "What shrieker here is trying to say is that he's glad mother made you ruler over us and this mission instead of us." Turning to the soldier it said, "Don't worry about them. We've been wanting freedom for so long that we can't wait to carry out our task." The soldier slowly nodded his head in understanding and confusion and walked away.

All this information was too much for Sirius. Too much, not that he could not comprehend it, but too much in the sense that he now regretted coming here alone. If he were ever caught, his actions up to now would all have been for nothing. Dying here would be a waste. And with no messenger bird, no paper to leave behind information and no one as good as him to track him down, he had to come out of this alive.

"Why is it again, that we must attack both castles at the same time?" asked the Cyclops.

"Because we don't know who exactly bears the key to the barrier. As the human historian called them, the descendants. But they'd likely be in ruling positions." Said the dragon in a rather annoying way.

"What about Nek? The humans captured it. Will we not go to its aid?" asked the Cyclops.

"Nek can free itself if it wants to. I am not worried about him. He has his mission. As soon as he can recognize the king. He'll call out to me." said Tish.

"Nek? Must be the four runner we captured. That means it was indeed a scout. Still a scout. A suicidal one. Come on John, Smith, Robert, sniff out the plot here. Come on Black, I know you can sense the danger coming. You have a gift for that. Stop drowning it in alcohol and sound the alarm. General, please, lift camp and head back to the castle." Thought Smith in an attempted communicative way.

No sooner was he done thinking so, Queen Erlen of Serdio woke up from a nightmare. A dream she knew not was real. Looking out the window, it was already late into the night. The castle was quiet. Walking up to it, she looked out to see a few torches lit down below the village surrounding the castle. "It doesn't look like a new day has started," said she. Looking back at her bed, she had no hope to see her husband. As always, he was probably drinking away with the generals and commanders. "Oh wait. The general is not here. Probably only the commanders then. Those boils on that man's skin, can it really be an epidemic? This is certainly too small of a task for a general. Yet too important of one it seems to leave behind his commanders."

Putting something more decent on, she went to the adjacent room connected with hers. There, laid asleep two baby girls and a nanny. Kissing one of the babies on the forehead she exited the room. *"I must check our archives. This dream, those creatures, I know I have seen them somewhere before. They can't be a figment of my imagination."*

Back at the border, Sirius was getting tired. Having been on the move for three days without sleep and only edible food found in the forest in his belly, he needed to lay down and rest. But doing so out in the open could reveal his position. He knew he did not snore. He always made sure of that. But if for some reason other creatures were to invade his surrounding, it will only take one to try and walk through the bush to see through his camouflage. He needs someplace high yet not too high, and dark enough to flip his cloak sides.

Without leaving his current position, he examined the forest behind him. The moon would soon show itself and that was another problem. Light passes through the empty spaces between leaves. His cloak would only create a shadow where there should be light. Scanning the trees, he saw one with a big hole in it. Moving as quietly and swiftly as possible he dashed it. Reaching it, he slowly removed his cloak and switched its side, revealing the underneath. It was of a dark color perfect to hide in the shadows.

Replacing it on his back and over his head, he climbed into the opening. It was the perfect hideout. Nighttime or daytime, it will be hard to know someone was hiding in there since neither sunlight nor moonlight could reach the inside. Pulling out his weapon as he was inside the tree, he made for himself a chair. By piercing his spear on the inside of the tree he anchored the tilt on the other side and sat on it. *"Now, if only I had some food."* Thought Sirius when something came dripping down his left cheek. Wiping it with his finder, he lifted it toward his nose. *"This is..."* putting his finger to his mouth, *"honey!"* Indeed, Sirius was inside a tree-filled from top to bottom with honey and with no bees in sight. *"No bees? That is odd. Could their presence be also affecting the normal function of insects?"* Sirius was referring to the presence of the dragon, cyclops, and shrieker.

It would soon be the fourth day since Sirius had undertaken this quest of his. To Smith, it was day three. While they, the lieutenants, were enjoying themselves with ales, Black had still not woken up. He slept all day all night. The laughter and commotion the other three lieutenants, John, Robert, and Smith, were making in the tent, was not affect his slumber. Rest he much needed. Black was the type of man, who never showed hints that something bothered him. So, annoying others and talking loudly was his way of drowning out his sorrow and hurt. But most importantly, drinking was his way of keeping his gift at bay.

A gift he was now unable to ignore since no ale was coursing through his blood. Black was trapped in his slumber the moment he fell asleep. Trap in his dream, unable to wake up. His mistake for thinking it will be a quick nap, then later in the afternoon, get drunk. A mistake that would turn to his benefit. For their survival. Consider it divine intervention. An intervention that wanted them to know what was going on. That wanted to warn them.

From the moment he fell asleep, the only thing he saw was total darkness. Such a dream was all too familiar. The type of sleep you wake up from and realize it was a dreamless one. That is until the moment Sirius made mention of his name from wherever he was. *"Come on Black, I know you can sense the danger coming. You have a gift for that. Stop drowning it in alcohol and sound the alarm. General, please, lift camp and head back to the castle."* The voice resonated inside his head.

"Sirius?" questioned Black in his sleep.

"Come on John, Robert, Black, we're in danger and so is the king. Get him back to the castle now. Serdio is soon to be under siege. We are next. And we are dealing with the likes we have never faced before. What we faced in the forest and field were but a before taste, the full course meal will annihilate us."

"Sirius is that you? Where are you?" Asked Black while still in his dream. Unbeknownst to him, he had been sleeping for twenty hours. He started to move about. He could feel the soft ground beneath his feet and the constant brushing of something or somethings against his arms and legs. That's when it hit him. He was not just asleep. This was something else. Something which he kept drowned at the bottom of jugs. He knew exactly what was there, though he could not see anything. This was not new. It only took for him to see it once, that he never wanted to see it again.

Black wanted to wake up, he did not want to go down that road again. This same road that cost him his father. Gifted as he is, his father sought to convince everyone that the warnings he received were, in fact, real. He was made a fool of and no one believed him. He was the town's mockery. In an effort to prove his sanity, he ventured into the dark forest. He crossed that barrier. It was unknown then, that not everyone could enter and that none would ever come out. No one knows what happened to his father, but he knew. He saw it. Every night. Over and over again. Like winter coming back every season.

Joining the army was his way of forgetting. Henri and Serdio, at that time, were having skirmishes along the borders, and men were needed. He climbed his way through the ranks and made friends as well as enemies. Enemies due to his anger back then. His rage for wanting it all to go away. Till that fateful night, he first tasted a real man's drink and fell into a slumber of nothingness. No memories, no visions, no death, no monsters, nothing. Just peace and a headache.

"Black." Came a voice from behind. A voice he did not want to turn around and see. He spent an eternity trying to forget and yet he recognized it after all these years. "Black, it's me." What the heck, he was no coward, not anymore.

"I'll face you today and will make sure to never see you again." Thought he, as he turned to face his dad.

"Hi, son. It's been a while." Said his father.

"You're dead, you shouldn't be here." Replied Black.

"And you should be awake safe and sound. Not here." Pitied his dad as he could feel the sorrow and hurt emitting from his son. "You did great Black. You are okay. Let it all go, son. Let it all go." Said he as he approached his son who burst in tears on his shoulders.

"Why are you here? Why now? I do not want to see your death again. I know what happened. That darkness swallowed you whole and burned you in the process. Why did you had to go? Why'd you have to try and prove yourself to everyone?" Sobbed Black.

"And why must you prove to everyone that you're just like them. Why hide your true self in duels, ales, foul mouths, and carelessness? It's ok Black. Don't fight it. Accept your gift. The sooner you accept it the better it gets. Sirius is calling out to you." Said his father.

"Sirius? Where is he?" asked Black

"He's not in camp where you are. He is in a dangerous place, surrounded by dangerous things. Among them, the thing you fear the most. The one I never saw coming, but only felt. Sharp teeth and fire. It is coming Black. You must warn everyone. Lift camp and run. Save the king, save the crown." Informed his dad, all the while backing away from his son and leaving him again in total darkness.

"*Black, Black, wake up! Warn Sirius. Can you see it? It is coming. Kill the four runner, do not let the king face it in battle.*" Black heard Sirius say yet with nothing or no one insight. Out of nowhere, a bright light appeared on his left. Behind it was a tree, with a hole, the size a man could fit through. Focusing on the hole within the tree, he could make a silhouette of a man pointing his finger at something. What the man was pointing at was right in front of him. No sooner did Black lay eyes on it, did it rush toward him. It rushed after Black with such speed that the only thing he had time to see and notices were two bright orange eyes belonging to a formless shadow. Followed by hot intense flames.

While everyone was having a great time, and easing to get some rest, Black was on his makeshift bed sweating.

Sweating not just normal sweat but sweat infuses with ale out of his system. The smell was strong enough that it caused Robert to ask, "all right, where's that hidden stash? Who held out on us?"

"Guys?" said John as he approached Black's sleeping body. Stupefy at what he was seeing. "Black?" called out he as he shook his sleeping companion's shoulder.

Jumping off the bed fully awake and gasping for air, Black woke up, startling everyone one present and causing them to take immediate distance from him. Breathing heavily, with single words in between breaths, Black said, "It's, coming. It got out."

CHAPTER 9

The Emergency

Getting up on his two feet, as if he were never asleep, he repeated, "It's coming. We have to move. The black demon, it got out."

"Hold your liquor, Black. It was only a nightmare. You can relax now. The cyclops are gone. You took care of them remember?" Said John, thinking Black woke up from a nightmare.

"No, you fool, this was no nightmare. You, just as I, know that something is not right here. This is bigger than cyclops. Bigger than those things the king faced. They are not even enough to qualify as a warm-up. What is coming is total annihilation. And after that, comes her. The End of all things." Said a hysteric Black as he paced back and forth, trying to persuade them of the urgency of the matter.

Robert and Smith stood there looking at each other. Almost as if wanting to communicate if Black, somehow sense what they had earlier during the day. By now the room reeked of alcohol. If you had entered the room, you would have thought someone spilled a barrel of ale on the floor. Neither of the three lieutenants present could grasp the meaning of what was happening. But if they knew one thing, it was that Black was no coward. And for him to be in such a state of panic, meant that there was some truth to what was happening to him.

Walking toward Black who was lost in thoughts and fear; fear of being called insane like his father was, Robert put a hand on his shoulder and said, "Tell us everything and fear not what we may think. I've seen many mysteries under the heavens, this will in no way be any different or weirder, nor the last."

Taking a seat on his bed, Black removed his soak shirt and asked for a clean one. After putting it on, he took a deep breath. "Sirius has been gone for four days..."

"Three," interjected Smith.

"Wrong, four. You only happen to realize he was not around after the first day of his departure. He is currently at the border, I think. He's been tracking down this creature." Informed Black.

"What kind of creature?" asked John.

"I don't know. I only know in parts. He is in a dangerous position, surrounded by the enemy. Three powerful ones. I did not see them. Only felt them. But the one among them I did see, is a terrible beast. The likes we cannot win against. That is all I could tell. And...," paused Black.

"And?" asked Robert.

"Sirius insists that the king is in danger and that we must get him out of here." Said Black. "Also," paused him, "Nek is waiting to identify the king."

"Who's Nek?" asked John.

Looking at Smith with wide eyes, Robert spoke up, "It's the four-runner," said he as both he and Smith got up in a sense of urgency, surprising Black.

Unknown to the lieutenants, Malvin and Edwin who had come to try and prove their worth to drink with the lieutenants, were listening at the tent's entrance. They did not need to hear anything else. The urgency in what they heard was enough. They had vital information for a report and with that, they ran to inform the king and general. Their reason for making haste was due to one fact only; on their way to join the lieutenants in their joyous evening fellowship, they had happened to see Philip and Bervard heading in the direction of Nek.

It would be a waste of time to inform the lieutenants. As they were still squabbling Black with questions. "How do you know all this? How is it you're communicating with Sirius?" they heard lieutenant John ask Black as they left.

"I DON'T KNOW, OKAY!" came forth a yelling and irritated answer from Black, who himself was not sure what to make of the knowledge he now knew and saw.

"We must make haste Edwin. If the situation turns dire, I am going to need you to stay back. You will have to report to the lieutenants if we are too late. Stay close behind me but be ready to run back on my command." Ordered Malvin.

"What? And let you get all the glory? Nonsense. If the king needs saving, you bet my name will be written among the legends for my bravery and deeds." Replied Edwin.

"Oh sure, you great and valiant messenger." Said a sarcastic Malvin. "Where's your weapon then?" questioned him as they both kept running to reach Philip and Bervard.

"Oh," was Edwin's reply as he realized he was unarmed. "Right then! I'll stay behind you."

They were far gone into the forest by the time the lieutenants made haste for the king's and general's tent. Black and Smith headed straight for Philip's tent, for he of the brothers would believe. Whereas John and Robert went to Bervard, with determination to tie him down if he refused to leave, even if it meant being charged with a capital offense against the crown.

Simultaneously arriving at their respective destinations, the lieutenants found no one inside. Regrouping in the middle of the camp, they realized how peaceful it was. Peaceful and restful. The soldiers, except for those on guard duties, were all asleep. It had been a very long four months. And this night, was their first freedom. Freedom from fear of being attacked, of constantly being on the move, of worrying their king would do something foolish. Unbeknownst to them, that foolishness was already on the verge of happening.

Philip, after having gotten a good amount of sleep, found himself unable to rest any longer. *"I bet a good old drinking jar of ale should fix this. Knowing them, I bet they're having some right now."* Thought Philip of his lieutenants. Getting up and out of his tent, he started walking toward their tent. "However, do they manage to sleep in each other's company without their being bloodshed is a mystery." Said Philip to himself. Reaching mid camp, Philip noticed a silhouette of someone sneaking through the forest in the direction of the four-runner. Without bothering to give it much thought, he knew who that had to be. Peering into one of the tents near him, Philip grabbed a sword and shield. "Can never be too careful," said he as he headed in the direction his brother took. "Maybe I shouldn't have rejected the throne. This is too much on these tired bones of mine." Said Philip as he realizes how much he has watched over his little brother the king. "But then again, it is my duty as a general. A double-edged sword indeed. I need a very long vacation. Just me, Audrey and Darrius. Oh, that would be lovely." By this point, Philip was mumbling to himself. The soldiers that were awake as he walked past their tents, wondering if their general was feeling okay.

Catching up with Bervard before he started his descent downhill toward the captured beast, he spoke up. "What are you up to brother?"

Startled that he was caught, Bervard remained cool and answered, "Nothing as you can see. I wanted to get a glimpse at what I'll be facing tomorrow."

"Oh really?" retorted Philip. "And you came to do just that well-armed I see." Referred Philip to Bervard's armor and weapons.

"As Smith always says, 'one can never be too careful' Philip. You would agree." Countered argued Bervard.

Being not in the mood to go another round of argument with his brother the king, Philip let it go. "Well as you can see, which you probably can't really under this darkened cloud covered mooned night sky, the beast is right in front of you. I would urge you not to get any closer to it, but you probably wouldn't listen."

"Why wouldn't you recommend that I do?" asked Bervard.

"Because dear brother, no matter how much pain we inflict it with, it barely flinches. It has about close to two dozen arrows in its body right now. It should be dead, but yet it lives." Said, Philip

"I see," responded Bervard, "all the more reason to get a better glance at it." Insisted Bervard.

Philip already tired with his brother was going to let him have whatever happens to him. He was not in the mood to watch over him tonight. If Bervard got attacked, he had resolved in his heart to do nothing. *"Maybe it is because I worry too much about you, that you refuse to change,"* thought Philip as he got ready to sit down on the cold grass floor. *"You want this? Then fine, by all means, assume its consequences."* Said he to his brother in his thoughts.

The king was nearing halfway toward the beast. He not only could now see the four runner, but he could also see the soldiers keeping watch on the other side of the tree lines. The moment Philip sat down, came from behind him, the sound of running footsteps. Taking it easy he turned around to find Edwin and Malvin.

"General quick, the king is in danger!" Both Malvin and Edwin said in unison. Alarmed and startled at what they said, for Bervard was right in front of him and in good shape, he could not quite comprehend where they were coming from. Malvin, looking around in the darkness, saw a figure approaching Nek. In wasting no time to explain the situation to Philip, he charged forward. Grabbing the person from the back by the collar of their armor, Malvin yanked him away.

The king, who was too busy and intrigued at seeing Nek, did not hear Malvin coming upon him. He woke up to his senses when he was pulled back. Not seeing the figure of his brother, Bervard wondered who in the whole camp would dare disrespect him so. Drawing out his sword in anger, he shouted, "what is the meaning of this soldier?" The king's shout was so loud in fact, that it woke up the guards who dozed off standing up.

Meanwhile, Edwin was not only busy explaining the situation to Philip, but also trying to stop him from intervening between Malvin and the king. "General, let Malvin handle the king. What you must know right now is of utter importance. We know death can await us for our actions, but it is necessary." Said Edwin to his general.

"What is the meaning of this? Answer me!" shouted the king again at his unruly subject.

"My king, I can't let you go any further. I know I am out of place to tell you what to do, but if you'd be so kind as to follow us back to camp, you'll find four of your lieutenants, who can better explain the situation than I." offered Malvin as an explanation.

Angry, but yet reserved, the king replied, "If they have something to tell me, they can come here. In fact, why don't you go get them for me; and if what they have to say is as important as you say, then your hands you get to keep."

"I cannot do that yo..." paused Malvin as he heard shuffling behind him. The beast was now awake, and he could feel its gaze on him. Surely, just as he heard Lieutenant Black saying, this creature was smarter than they gave it credit for. It was unclear as to how it could recognize the king. But one thing was certain, he needed to get Bervard away from here. "I cannot do that Bervard. You must leave this place at once or else I'll have to drag you out myself." Dare Malvin, as he could not take a chance on formality.

Stopping Edwin in his speech, who just about told him what Black had seen, Philip heard Malvin's capital offense as did Edwin. They were both shocked. Taking steps forward to call his soldier in line, Edwin once again stopped him. Quickly analyzing the situation, he explained to Philip. "The range of this creature intelligence shouldn't be challenged nor taken for granted. We can't risk addressing each other formally." Said Edwin.

"Am I to overlook Malvin's offense toward his highness?" questioned Philip as he continued his walk toward Bervard.

Edwin could feel anger swelling up in him. Why couldn't any of them grasp the situation? It looked just like pride before a fall and stubbornness that lead to death. Or the pending doom, that cannot but happen despite all the warnings. Picking up his courage, he ran toward Philip. Grabbing him, also by the collar, he yelled in his face, "listen to reason would you, we need to get him out of here." Edwin's voice was even louder than the king's. Loud enough to be heard by the lieutenants entering the forest.

By the time the lieutenants got there, they witnessed a scene of violence. Edwin, whom they could not identify in the darkness, was on the ground and Philip had the tip of a sword in front of his throat ready to strike; and far below were two figures battling it out with swords. The commotion was getting vivid and loud, that by now, the protocol was broken and the whole camp was lighted and heading in their direction.

By the time torches made their way to their locations, and the area was well lit, everyone could see Edwin the messenger running away from Philip's sword; and Philip who with every strike, was intent on killing. Looking down below, Robert saw the other two figures were the king and Malvin. The kid was holding his own against the king.

As soon as the place was well lit, Nek, after analyzing the situation went about to accomplish his mission. Standing upon its two hind legs, it proceeded to alert the enemy, its comrade. With a mixture of a shriek and a yell, it went about producing the most horrifying and deafening sound ever; and with it came a burst of wind, having as its center Nek, that spread outwards towards the forest and taking with it the creatures screeching call.

"Smith," called out Robert, "aim for the throat, quick!" yelled him throughout the noise. Smith who always carried his weapons on him, took out his bow and arrow and aimed at the beast. So precise and powerful was the strike that it went straight through the beast's vocal cords. And yet so loud was Nek that the after effect left everyone's ears ringing. As all those present regained their composure, and both the king and Philip had stopped their nonsense, everyone witnessed the beast falling over on its side. Not as a newly killed beast, but as a rigor mortis corpse. If that was not strange enough, another sound was heard reverberating throughout the forest. It was not anywhere near them, but loud enough was it to be heard. And with it came not a returning gust of wind, but a breeze. A cold killer breeze.

Looking to Black, John saw him fighting to stay standing as he wiped blood dripping from his nose. "We're too late," Black told him as he dropped unconscious on the floor.

CHAPTER 10

The Stubbornness of a King

"Black?!" yelled John as he rushed toward him. Raising his head off the floor, he lightly taps his cheeks in hope that he would regain consciousness. "Wake up Black! We need you. What's coming? What was that noise? Come on Black, wake up!"

Getting their composure back, Bervard and Philip both stopped fighting. Philip's face showed signs of remorse for what he tried to do to, to a now petrified Edwin. "I'm sorry," was all he could muster to his subordinate as he turned his back on him and headed in the direction of the king.

King Bervard, was a different story. His face and demeanor along with body language, all showed signs that this was not over. Malvin knew this. Taking a couple of steps away from his king, Malvin did not dare for once sheath back his sword. With swords still in hand both allies, now turned enemies, backed away from the other with caution. Bervard, advancing backward towards Nek corpse to inspect it, did not dare for once turn his back toward Malvin. Not because he feared the young lad would strike, but because he wanted to make sure Malvin knew that this was far from over. Malvin did the same, but not for the same reasons as the king. He knew he was now an enemy of the king and any opportunity given, the king would take it.

Approaching from behind, Philip tap Malvin's shoulders. Startled, Malvin turned to see a downcast general. "Join Robert and stay by his side," said he to Malvin. Continuing his walk toward king Bervard, together they inspected the dead creature's corpse. There were no signs of blood from its recent wounds. Not even from the arrow that went straight through its vocal cord. It was as if it died years ago and the remains were preserved.

"What do we do?" asked John of the other lieutenants as limited time was all they had.

Rejoining Robert, Malvin, looked to him for orders, "Robert?"

"I'd say we abandon camp. We take only essentials, weapons. The rest we leave behind." Advised Robert. "John you go and convince the king to lift camp. He will not want to leave. In his current state, any orders he gives will be our doom. Tell him we will head for the castle and will have whatever is out there coming for us, chase us to it. If he asks why, tell him it is so that everyone can witness his glory and might. In other words, tickle his ego. Smith, in the meantime, debrief Philip on the side. Whatever is on its way here, we are no match for. Tell him," Robert thought about threatening to break rank, "tell him all that Black told us. But be brief we don't have time."

With that, both lieutenants departed to fulfill their comrade orders. Robert stayed with Black who was still unconscious and whose nose now started to bleed. Malvin who was now far from danger put away his sword and wondered if he did the right thing. "You did what you could Malvin." Robert interrupted. "This is not your fault. The fault is mine and Smith for sensing something was not right and yet saying nothing about it. And if Nek was the one sent to assassinate the king, you did well keeping him far from it."

Although Robert was right, Malvin was unable to feel guiltless. Guilt not for the king, but Robert. He saw it before, and it was bought to happen again. Robert was nearing the point of no return. He was becoming that man, that torturer that he witnessed in that forest years ago. The way Robert was staring at the king said it all. And he knew exactly what was going on in his mind. Vengeance. Scenes of torture. Of revenge. If ever the king did or manages to do what he sought to do just now *to me, you'll kill him without hesitating. Wouldn't you, Robert? Papa?"* That's what Robert was really to him. Though they were not related, he cared more for him than his previous father; and his wife's kindness reminded Malvin of his mother. "You promised Robert. You promised." Said Malvin, referring to Roberts' promise to never go dark again.

"Countless men have died because of his follies of glory. You shall not be one of them. I will end him if he ever tries. This I swear to you." Said Robert as he raised his head to look up at Malvin.

"Why do you let out tears? I'm alive. That is all that matters." Comforted Malvin. "Dry your eyes, Robert, the battle has just begun. Something's coming and we need to move fast."

"Edwin!" yelled out Robert. Approaching the lieutenant, Robert spoke up. "Wake up camp. This is a top priority. They are to take only their weapons. Leave tents, spoils, and games behind. No torches are to be lit. Is that understood?"

"Yes Sir!" Exclaimed Edwin.

"Good! Also, bring our weapons to us. Make haste lad, make haste." Ordered Robert to an already speedy messenger shouting orders to the men with lit torches surrounding them. "Malvin, you stay here with Black. Staying here any longer is senseless."

"What are you going to do?" asked a concerned Malvin.

"What must be done." Was Robert's reply as he got up to go join the other lieutenants. Kneeling with knees to the floor, Malvin placed Black's head on his thighs. Staring at Robert's back, he hoped for the best.

Robert was collected but fierce in his walk. He walked as one with authority. His facial countenance resembled that of a man heading to war and at peace with the circumstances. Of the soldiers present, though Malvin noticed it first, they could sense danger and war emitting from Robert. But there wasn't any bloodlust. At least not yet. All depended on what the king would say and do next.

King Bervard had his back toward Robert as he was listening and discussing, to him, the absurdity of what the lieutenants were reporting. No one present, not Philip his brother nor the two lieutenants, John and Smith, had to tell the king of the potential trouble approaching from behind. The king felt its every intention. Intentions for revenge.

Having had Smith across from him, Bervard walked toward him and turned around to face the newcomer. Putting Smith between himself and the person with the strong urge for revenge, he found it to be Robert. It did not take much for the king to realize his folly in wanting to judge Malvin. At least, now he noticed his folly because of the man he saw and felt before him.

It was not so much as the fear that silent the king. More so that he saw in Robert, this new Robert, a challenger he would much rather have on his side than that of the enemy.

"Robert?" Said the king. "Are you here for revenge?"

Ignoring the king, Robert questioned Philip. "What's the plan? Are we lifting camp or not?" Brief and dry was his question.

Having been brief by Sirius these many years ago of what Robert was capable of, Philip was careful to choose his words. "We are discussing this as we speak. If we are not to lift camp, it will be best to send the sick and wounded back to the capital. As for the rest of us, we'll anchor down and prepare ...."

"And prepare what?" Said an angry Robert. "Prepare for more men to die, because you won't listen to reason?" Turning to the king he continued, "Because Black's warning seems absurd and unreal? What we killed these past four months were supposed to be unreal. And yet they exist, along with a darkened forest no one can see through." Yelled Robert. "If you want to stay and fight, by all means, stay. But my men are coming with me. With or without your permission your highness."

Of the lieutenants and Philip, none knew why the king stayed silent at his subordinate lack of respect. Was it fear? Did his consciousness kick in? It was a mystery. "Philip, we're lifting camp. Leave everything behind, we're traveling light." Said Bervard.

"I've already given that order. All that awaits is for us to get ready." Confessed Robert as he stared sternly at the king. Staring back at him, Bervard said nothing. In a showdown of stares, the king finally moved from his position. Brushing his shoulder against Robert he headed toward camp or rather what was going to be left of it.

The atmosphere was intense. It resembled that of two sovereign states on the verge of signing a fragile peace treaty, this was not over. From now on it was their duty to keep Robert and the king apart or at the very least, not alone.

As the lieutenants and general were studying their comrade subordination, Malvin approached lieutenant general from behind. Wasting no time, Malvin raised his fist and punched Robert on the back of his head. Surprise and in shock "ouch" were his only response as he laid a hand where he was hit. "What was that for?" asked Robert as he turned to see who it was.

"That was to make sure you don't do or think of anything stupid." Replied the young Malvin as he punched Robert again, but lightly, on the shoulder. To which Robert smiled and walked away. The now four men in arms watched as Robert picked Black's unconscious body off the floor unto his shoulders. Looking back at his spectators Robert asked, "You guys coming or what?" and immediately after continuing his walk to exit the area, heading back to camp.

As if it was planned and timed, Philip, Smith, and John, exhaled loudly in relief.

Wanting to be sarcastic, Malvin looked at them and asked, "What was that about?" But before they could respond he left their company running toward Robert.

"Is he for real?" asked Smith, "Did he not see what could have happened?"

"He knows." Reassured John. "That's his way of making light of the situation."

"Whatever happens from now on John, you ride with Robert. You are not to leave him out of your sight. Smith, you take care of Black. Once we get back to the capital, I'll send a search and rescue for Sirius." Said Philip.

"What about you? What are you going to do?" asked John.

"I'll take care of the king." Said Philip as he waved the rest of the soldiers out the forest.

Nearing the camp, Robert saw no sign of the King. He was not looking for him, nor did he need anything from him. But he now could not help but think of ways the king might sneak up on him to strike. Glancing back, he saw Malvin walking behind him from a distance, eyeing the tree lines. *"Smart lad." Thought Robert. "You catch on quick."*

It was not that they were sure the king would go to such lengths. But the priority now was to get everyone to safety, royalty included. It was their duty as soldiers.

"He's not going to strike you know." The voice startled Robert. "He's in his tent packing up. Don't ask me how I know. I just do. You know just as I, that he is not heartless. You are too protective of Malvin. That's the issue." Said Black.

"Glad to hear you're awake." Said Robert as he continued walking.

"I am fully awake and in need to piss. So, if you would be so kind as to let me down, I would appreciate it. Unless of course, you don't mind me going while on your back?" said Black.

At those words, Robert did not hesitate to drop Black to the floor.

"Ouch, ouch, ouch. I say put down, not drop down." Complained Black as he got up. Finding the nearest tree, he proceeded to empty his bladder.

"I presume you have good news and bad news?" questioned Robert as Malvin joined in.

"I don't know which it is." Said Black as he tightened his belt to face Robert and Malvin. "Sirius has bought us time. He struck the dragon in the mouth. Seems it was vulnerable there. The good news for us is that we now have more time to escape."

"What's the bad news?" asked Malvin.

"The bad news is that Sirius just committed suicide by revealing his presence." Said, Robert.

"They don't know where he is." Confirmed Black.

"Doesn't matter. The very fact that Sirius attacked puts him at a disadvantage. He heard everything they were plotting and now, they'll be on the hunt for him." Said Robert with regret. "Is that all you saw?"

"Nope." Said Black. The moment he responded, something came crashing down behind him sending smoke, dirt, and debris up in the air. This of course caught Robert and Malvin off guard, along with everyone else in the forest. Smith and John along with Philip made haste to the location where the sound came from. King Bervard ran out of his tent and seeing the smoke made haste toward its location, and the rest of the camp pursued.

As the surrounding was yet still dusty, Robert heard Philip calling from behind. "I am over here." He responded. It was not yet clear, but Black seemed to still have his back toward what crash behind him. *What the hell is going on?* thought Robert.

Faintly making out a shape among the smoke. The creature, or so it seemed rose in heights. It was about the heights of the pine trees. Easily 50 to 60 feet tall. And with that, as with the sound, they had heard early, that resonated far away in response to Nek's call, so was this same sound accompanied with flames.

"Black, what did you do?" questioned Robert.

CHAPTER 11

Newcomer, Friend or Foe?

Black sensed an uneasiness as he and the other lieutenants exited the tent. Was it because they believed every word he told them? He was not sure. But one certain thing was the fact that they did not treat him like people did his dad. After years of drowning out this gift of his, it felt foreign and new. Crazy he wasn't, and he was glad his comrades thought no less of him.

"Let's split up," said John. "Smith, you and Black go to the general. He of the two will most likely be willing to listen and believe. Robert and I we'll inform the king."

"Alright. I would say it will be crucial at this stage, especially not knowing what will happen, to wake up camp. Let's avoid causing a panic, though. It will be best to be on guard. We don't know what else may be coming or is already here." suggested Smith, as he raised his eyes toward the treetops, referring to the one eye treehoppers.

"I agree. Best to be expecting a war than to be surprised by one." agreed Robert.

"Guys were wasting time. We need to move now." interjected a cautious Black.

With determination, they departed from each other to carry out their missions. On the way to Philip's tent, Smith would, with every soldier he crossed path with, order them to wake camp and have them prepare for imminent danger. When they got to Philip's tent, it was empty. Turning to the guard outside the general's tent, Black questioned, "where's the general?"

"The general went to see his majesty, sir." replied the guard.

Looking at each other, Smith and Black double back and made haste to reach the king's tent. Getting halfway there, for Philip's tent was on the other side of camp across from the king's, they met with Robert and John. "Where's the king?" asked Smith.

"He wasn't in his tent," answered Robert.

"Neither was the general," informed Smith.

By now, the camp was getting lively and noisy again. Frustration could be seen on the faces of some for lack of sleep, others were just tired and ready to go home.

"Has anybody seen the king and general?" yelled John as his impatience started kicking in.

"Lieutenants," step forth a soldier, "I don't know about the king, but the general took my sword and shield from my tent minutes ago."

"Where did he go?" pressed on John.

"I saw him head toward the forest. More precisely in the direction of that creature we captured." informed the soldier.

Wasting no time to know more, they ran in after the general. They knew their general was not the foolish type.

If he went in armed at this time of night, it must mean he is with the king. There was no time to waste. This was priority number one.

Approaching the forest, they heard someone yell these words, 'listen to reason would you, we need to get him out of here.' "Who could that be I wonder?" asked Smith as they came to a complete stop.

"Let's not wait to find out," replied John.

As they race to reach the king and Philip, as well as whoever else was there, none noticed Black fighting to keep up. He was profusely sweating. He seems like someone fighting death itself. But keeping up he did. Having made it three-quarters of the way, they heard swords clashing. As well as someone soberly begging, "general stop! We have to leave immediately!"

No sooner than they heard these words, that they saw a guard zoom past them heading back to camp, shouting, "torches, light up your torches. We need more light!"

Reaching their destination, the lieutenants were profoundly uncertain as to what was happening. Not too far before them, was a man with a sword trying to kill another that kept dodging every strike. Beyond them, were two others battling it out with their swords. The guards keeping an eye out on Nek had their torches lit, but being where they were, it was still hard to tell who these fighters were. Frozen and not knowing what to do, time flew by fast for soldiers came around toward their location with lit torches. Lighting everything, they could not see.

Edwin was on the floor at the mercy of the general's sword, whose tip was underneath his chin. Whereas as Malvin was holding his own against king Bervard, giving him no opening to exploit. At seeing this Robert was relieved but more so proud of his captain's abilities. However, that contentment was short-lived, and a good thing for Edwin. Analyzing the situation, Nek rose on its hind legs and went about producing the most horrid and terrifying sound ever heard by man.

Spreading out through the forest like the force of an explosion, Nek's horrid shriek, left everyone's ear ringing. At Robert's order, Smith had aimed for the beast's vocal cord, putting an end to its loudness. Smith looked to Robert, with a nod thank him for his quick actions. As everyone was regaining their composure, a roar of a mighty beast was heard coming from across the land, accompanied by a cold killer breeze. Eyeing each other, Black's gazes fell upon John's as he said, "We're too late," before fainting.

King Bervard and General Philip regained their sanity as they cease fighting. Looking to Edwin who was too stunned and scared to move, the only thing Philip found to say to express his regret, was, "I'm sorry." Heading toward his brother the king, he wondered how and, *why did this have to happen?"* Looking at Malvin, he could not help but see a scenario where the kingdom fell apart. Glancing back, Philip could see all four lieutenants and the soldiers that had gathered. Eyeing Robert specifically, he saw nothing but blood. Indeed, and it would only take but one life to set the chaos in motion. Malvin's. Tapping the young captain on the shoulders, Philip ordered him to rejoin Robert's side. Philip heard John's constant calls begging Black to wake up.

"That could wait for now," thought he. Right now, his priority was to be by his brother, the king's side.

Black knew what was happening to him. At least he had a hint. He was going to faint and see something he probably did not want to. What he feared the most, was waking up surrounded by enemies. The stakes being so high, this was now out of his control. And if he could save everyone with this gift of his, then he would gladly run the risks. Giving in to his gift, he fell unconscious as he heard John's voice distancing far from him. Waking up he found himself on the floor. Raising himself, he felt the grass underneath his hands. He was in a forest. Looking up and around him, he was right. Trees were surrounding him.

With his senses coming back, he heard a commotion in a dark spot in the forest. Focusing on it he noticed it was retreating. Exploring his environment, he found the tree Sirius had hidden in. Approaching it, he was not prepared for what he was about to see. The inside of the tree was splattered with blood. Knowing this was Sirius hideout, he was not sure what to think. To him and the other lieutenants, Sirius was not much of a fighter and so feared that what he was looking at was the remains of his comrade. Looking up at the interior of the tree, he saw Sirius's cloak. Pulling it free, he folded it against his chest. The cloak was not soaking wet with blood. It was dry. Desert dry, with no taint of blood. "What is the meaning of this?" asked Black. Laying his hand against the blood tainted interior of the tree, he peered his head inside it once more, expecting to possibly see his comrade, he found no one.

His hand had made contact with the blood, caused him to have a vision. It was a vision within a vision. Like a dream within a dream. A vision that took him back to what happened.

"I am starving." Black saw shrieker say. "Where's the nearest village, soldier?"

"It's about ten minutes or so from here," answered the soldier.

"Is everyone there alive or dead?" asked the creature.

"There are some survivors we're keeping prisoners." informed the soldier.

"Where's your general?" asked shrieker.

"He's headed for the castle to attack it from the inside with his men, sir... creature, sir." responded the soldier, confused at what to call the thing questioning him."

Looking at Tish and cyclops, the shrieker said, "I'll be right back," in a sweet creepy voice.

A couple of minutes later, it returned with living people. Living villagers, that it had impaled with his claws. Black did not have time to count how many they were, as the creature wasted no time in scrapping them from its nails onto the floor, one over the other. The last villager to fall was a young boy. Getting up terrified at the sight of the three beings he saw before him, he tried to run. But due to his injuries, he could not. All he could do was try to escape. Shrieker did not bother with the young lad as he started to feast one after the other on the villagers before him.

Screaming in agony and begging for their lives as they were devoured by the beast. When the boy would be out of reach of his claws and arms, shrieker would smack yank him, back at its feet.

Black could not watch any longer. He wished he could help, but alas what he was seeing had already occurred. Hiding his eyes and shielding his ears, he tried to drown out the sufferings and calls for rescue from the villagers. In the meantime, the young lad tried several times to escape, but each time producing the same results. He was back at the creature's feet. He did not want to die; he did not want to be eaten. Having noticed the tree, where Sirius was hiding in, he dashed it. Shrieker seeing the direction the boy was heading in, let him.

Reaching the tree, the boy looked up inside to see Sirius. "Help me, please. I am begging you, please help me." cried him, as he held out his arms toward Sirius as he tried to climb inside. It was the lad's cry for help that caused Black to reopen his eyes. Seeing where he was and knowing Sirius was inside, he was curious to see what happened next. Having successfully, but painfully climb inside, he kept repeating his pleas for help. But alas, against such foes Sirius could not give away his position. Black who was not so far off, got closer to the tree to see what was happening. Sirius had turned his back on the boy, who was now crying in desperation as he watched Shrieker get closer.

"Come out human. I promise to eat you very slowly you lively jittery meal," said Shrieker as he got closer and closer. "If you come out now, the sooner you get to die," laughed the evil creature.

Clinging to Sirius cloak, the young lad climbed. He climbed and brought his face right up to Sirius'. With such innocence, soft tone desperate voice, that no tyrant could ever ignore, he said to Sirius, "please help me," before closing his eyes.

"Have your way then," said Shrieker as it went about piercing the tree very slowly. Seeing the trajectory of the enemy's nails, Sirius pulled out his dagger. He had a decision to make. Help this boy out and risk detection and vital information or leave things to fate. The decision to help the boy out, righteous and good as it seems, would mean losing the element of foreknowledge. Knowledge of what their plans were for both kingdoms and the devastation and annihilation to come. Resisting with all his might, he chose, the hardest, yet wisest decision he deemed necessary.

"Please, please help," whispered the boy, as his life started to leave him. With the shriekers nail still digging in through the tree, about to pin the boy down and impale him a second time. This time to the chest and painful would it be. Pulling the lads head against his chest, he whispered back, "I got you. I've got you," before plunging his dagger through the boy's heart. "I've got you. You can rest now. He won't get, he can't get you now." Comforted Sirius. With his last breath, the passing lad said his last words, "thank you," before his impalement.

Not hearing any screams from his prey, the shrieker removed his nails as a lifeless body fell in the opening of the tree. Angry that his last prey was lifeless and dead, shrieker with anger went about mutilating the boy's body before eating the remains.

"You have to be strong Sirius. This is no time to be crying. This is nothing compared to what maybe if they have their way." Sirius was motivating himself, trying not to think of what he just did.

The cyclops and the dragon did not budge. Nor did they show signs of wanting what the Shrieker was eating. They only looked on emotionless as they awaited the call to start their mission. A call, a sign, which came in the form of Nek's scream. Upon hearing it, the three beasts readied themselves.

"Finally," exclaimed cyclops.

"The time has come. As planned, you guys will storm the castle of Serdio, and I will take care of Henri," said Tish.

"Why must you get Henri to yourself?" Complained Shrieker.

"Their country is smaller than Serdio. No need to divide our forces and risk the other dragons, if any still live, and nations coming to this land's aid." Explained Tish. "Annihilate them all. Bring their kingdom to the ground. Leave no royals, nor castle standing."

"With pleasure." Smiled Cyclops as he turned his back on Tish and headed toward Serdio, followed by Shrieker. As they left Tish's presence, the forest before them lit up. Sirius could not believe there were hundreds, if not thousands of soldiers just a stone throws away from him. And to think he made it within enemy camp without being noticed. This was certainly not a chance, nor luck. It had to be a miracle.

Raising his head in the air, spreading its wings, Tish took to show his dominance and his return by replying to Nek's call, with his roar. The dragon's roar shook the very ground Black was standing on. The whole forest was paralyzed and trembled at the presence of such evil. Though it was only a vision, Black took cover behind a tree. But one did not tremble, one did not fear. Did not fear dying. Did not fear risking it all here, not anymore. Pulling his bow and arrow, Sirius prepared to aim. Using the retreating soldiers' torches as light, though faint, Sirius peered the tip of his arrow through the hole shrieker's nail had made. Aiming for Tish's heart, or at least where he thinks the heart is, he steadied his hands. Sirius was on the verge of releasing the arrow but remembered the dragon's conversation with the other beasts. More especially, Shrieker.

"It said, its nails and claws were worthless against him. Therefore, so will be my arrows." realized Sirius. "In that case, I doubt your inside is as tough as your outer skin." Said he as he released his arrow. Sirius watched as his arrow hit its mark. Striking Tish in the mouth and landing and piercing its upper mouth, the beast went into a rage of hurt, stopping it short in its roar. Spitting out a constant flow of flames, the dragon ended up burning the wooden part of the arrow.

In all this, Black felt useless. All he could do was watch. Watching, now, in fear that Sirius may have just given away his position. Tish was so out of control, that his flame not only set ablaze a couple of trees, but it also halted the mission. However, the chaos was short-lived. Bearing through the pain, Tish controlled himself.

"What is the meaning of this? A forest fire is not part of the plan!" Yelled Cyclops as he ran toward Tish.

Ignoring Cyclops and the incoming, Shrieker, Tish used his claws to dig out the remnants of whatever struck him in the mouth. Being unable to, it resorted to asking Shrieker for help. "Shrieker, get over here. I need your help. I need your claws."

Calling a soldier with a torch to come to his side, Shrieker peered its head inside Tish's mouth. "You're bleeding," said Shrieker. "Not so invulnerable on the inside I see." Said it a somewhat menacing way.

Tish responded with an equal threat, "you're in a perfect position to lose your head. Let me know when you want to be headless, and I'll deliver the blow."

Pulling out, not one, but two arrowheads, Shrieker revealed them to Tish. Taking just a glance at them, Tish said severely, "we have a traitor in our mists, find him."

"What is the meaning of this?" Came a strolling commanding Serdian officer on horseback. "Everything and everyone are ready. We can't delay any longer."

Showing the officer the metal arrowheads, the officer wasted no time to issue orders for the surrounding forest to be searched. If there's a spy, I can assure you, it's none of my men. Having noticed the tree where Sirius is hiding in, the officer proceeded to check it out himself. Grabbing a torch from a nearby soldier, he drew his sword. Upon approaching the tree, he saw the carnage that remained. "What happened here?" questioned him.

Having heard his question, Shrieker replied, "Oh, that was just a little snack," as it giggled.

Peering the torch inside the hollow tree, the officer proceeded to inspect it. Looking inside he found nothing but the remains of honey. Angry, yet collected, he said, "we can't waste time like this. Everyone, forward. The general is waiting for us, we can't delay any longer.

No one, not even Black noticed when Sirius got out. "You are the best tracker and spy after all. And to think I was worried about you." Said Black to himself. Turning around to see if he could spot Sirius, Black froze as he heard a voice calling for a peculiar name he had not heard in ages.

"Ironclad? Ironclad, where are you? Their coming. Did you warn them, as I had instructed you to?"

Slowly turning his head, Black watched as his current location raced beneath his feet. He was no longer surrounded by the enemy. Nor night for that matter. It was sunrise, and his current location was in a plain somewhere.

"Ironclad, why aren't you talking? Have you forgotten me after all these years?" came forth a voice above him. Looking up, Black watched as a dragon flew, then landed before him. It resumed talking, "you sure smell and look like Ironclad, but the ironclad I know should be much older. Who are you, stranger?" It asked Black.

"You can see me?" asked Black in shock.

To which the dragon answered with a nod and asked, "where is Ironclad? This is urgent."

"I am Ironclad. Black Ironclad. How did you know my father?" asked Black in shock.

CHAPTER 12

Wake Him Up

Reaching the royal chambers of history, with a torch in hand, Queen Erlen set out to consult the ancient scrolls. Reading through the kingdoms' entire history, she could not find what she was looking for. No scrolls made mention of the crest on her back, there was nothing about dragons and very few details concerning what was hidden and trapped within the dark forest.

"That can't be. I remember my father showing me them. They exist, I just know they do." said Erlen frustratingly that it's taking this long. Running across the room, she decides to consult every shelf. Looking through records of trade, of war, of territory. Still, she could not find what she wanted. "Don't tell me, that fool had them destroyed?" asked Erlen out loud, about her husband the king. Having spent hours in the library, a lifetime of emotions was streaming down her cheeks. Emotions of disappointment and misunderstanding, fused with constantly being called crazy by her husband, all piled up into tears as she wished for someone to be by her side. To be there with her in her search for answers and truth.

Feeling hopeless and abandon, queen Erlen sat down in hopelessness; contemplating an old tapestry hung on the far side of the room. It was secluded all by itself. With no light, other than the torch in her hand, to show her great, great grandfather's tapestry, it was partly engulfed in shadows. And that is exactly how she felt at that moment. She remembered her father's story concerning it.

"What do you think it is?" She recalled her dad once asked her.

"I don't know. It looks like a giant rock." her eight-year-old, self-had replied.

"What you are looking at is a dragon. I know it doesn't look like one, but it is." had said her father.

"That's a dragon?" laughed young Erlen.

"Yes, dear! That is a dragon. A dragon in slumber. There's no way for you to tell by the painting, I know. But my great grandfather painted this after his encounter with the beast. And ever since, he would not stop saying that a dragon was living inside the castle walls. The good thing is, back then he was no longer king. My grandfather was. So, everybody assumed he was starting to lose his mind due to old age." said her dad.

"Did you, grandpa and great grandpapa believe him, dad?" asked Erlen.

Looking down at her daughter, the previous king smiled, "of course we did. Just as I know you believe me. You now bear the mark of such truth and many more. And later in life, you shall pass it on to your firstborn. Just as I have with you." said her father.

"Then where's the dragon?" had asked Erlen.

"That I cannot tell you, sweetheart. Many a mystery there are in this world. Some can be told. Others must be discovered. Just like this one. You must find it. You must find him. But do not look for him when you do not need him. When the time comes, and I feared it will come in your reign, seek him out. Wake him up. Wake him up and command him. A day will come when this tapestry shall crumple of age. Then, only then, shall you find what must be found."

Growing up, that is not what she had imagined her future would be. That is not what she had hoped for her kingdom. It was falling apart, and her foolish husband, did nothing if little to change this. In anger of her current predicament and at her father doing little to prepare her for this, she grabbed her torch and threw it at the family painting. Successfully setting it ablaze. She watched as the flames consumed the image of the so-called dragon. "A dragon you once told me. To be honest, it still looks like a giant rock." queen Erlen said out loud.

And as that rock burned, the flames spread outwards, toward the edges of the tapestry. Thus, leaving a giant dark hole in the middle. A hole, thanks to the light provided by the flames, should have been square-shaped rocks. As more of the tapestry burned, the more was revealed. As if to say behind that tapestry was a secret passage not lit for years. Surprised and cautious, her father's words now made sense to her, *"A day will come when this tapestry shall crumple of age. Then, only then, shall you find what must be found."* As well as that of her great, great grandfather, *"a dragon lives inside the castle walls."*

Rushing forward, she picked up her torch where it landed and stood back waiting for the tapestry to burn completely all the while trying to hold back her excitement. Once it was all ashes, the size of the entrance wall was wide enough for three fat cows to fit in together. The opening was a clean cut through the wall. Peering her torch through, she could see the floor on the other side. Holding the torch above her, the ceiling was nowhere near visible. "Could this be a cave? This deep below the castle?"

"Wake him up. Wake him up and command him." Her father's voice echoed in her head. Taking up courage, she walked through to the other side with confidence. Like the queen that she is, she walked with boldness. With the strength and courage required of her, of her crowned, she feared not the darkness around her. Having walked a great distance from the room of records, with her back toward it, and darkness before her, she raised her voice, "dragon of old, it is I your queen." Her voice echoed throughout the darkness, but nothing responded.

Raising her voice, a second time she said, "dragon of old, wake up, for your queen summons you!" Still no response. *"Call him out."* she heard her dad's familiar voice. Taking in a deep breath, and this time with full authority she spoke firmly, "My name is Queen Erlen of Henri. Heir to my father's throne, and his forefathers before him. I command thee to heed my call. By the power of this crest, I command thee to wake up!" she raised her voice at the end. And as the echo of her voice died down, the familiar noise of cracking echoed back. Faintly at first, then louder and louder until it stopped altogether.

Waiting in total silence and not knowing what to expect, Queen Erlen wondered whether she was brave or foolish to be down here all alone. Placing her lit torch ahead above her head, she took a couple of steps forward. With every step echoing throughout this unknown territory. On her fifth step, a low growl was heard, causing her to stop advancing. Awaiting the worst, she listened as something shuffled in the shadows. Shuffled and approaching.

She could feel something was there in front of her. She could feel it but could not see anything. Grasping her hands around the torch, she threw it as far as she could in front of her. She watched as the torch spun in mid-air and yet still not bright enough to let her see what was around her in the darkness. But when it landed on the floor, it was clear to see what was facing her. Shocked and afraid, Erlen started to pace back toward the room of records, back to where it was better lit.

Having fallen away from her, as she intended, the flames of her once held torch, revealed claws the length of a fox and halfway below her knee in height. No painting was necessary to help her make sense of what she was seeing. As soon as she saw the claws, queen Erlen took her first step back. As she did so a wind, or rather a breath, blew out her only light source. Now in total darkness, she kept her pace and tried not to panic. With every step she took, it felt like the dragon was taken twenty of his own. And as she reached the entrance she once crossed; the dragon's breath was beating down on her head. Slowly but surely, she crossed back to her domain, her familiar territory, as she heard shuffling noises once more through the dark cave. Running toward the stairwells, she unhooks a fresh torch off the wall. Pacing back to where she once stood, she watched as the dragon's scale became visible. It was dark gray. Without expectations, what she was looking at, flung open, and a giant eyeball stared back at her. Dirty orange was the color of its eye. That was the last thing Erlen saw before fainting.

When she woke up, it took her a couple of seconds to figure out where she was. Whether inside the room of records or in the dragon's cave. For, there were no lid sources anywhere. Sitting up she tried to adjust her eyes to the darkness around her. But alas, in vain.

"Queen of Henri, how is your father?" asked a deep tone voice.

Hesitating to answer, Queen Erlen answered anyway, "My, father, my father passed away, many years ago. How did you know him?" asked her, somewhat already knowing the answer to her question.

"Just as I knew his father, and the one before that, for as long as the line of your descendants made resident in these lands." answered the voice.

"Wait, how old must you be? How old can dragons live to be?" asked Erlen as she got off the floor.

"I am old. I was old and was no more. And then, I became again. And soon, I'll be no more." answered the dragon.

"Well, that doesn't answer my question." Thinking of a better question she asked, "you said, my descendants, came to these lands. Where were they from?"

"They came from across the vast lands of water," said the dragon.

"You mean the ocean. Who were they, do you know? Or remember?" asked Erlen.

"Who they were, I know not. But what they became, that I know. And you are the same as them. You are a guardian. The first line of defense, against what lies in our prison. A prison me and my kind created." revealed the dragon.

"Well, your prison isn't what it used to be. Creatures of unknown origins have been killed roaming our lands. Entire villagers near it have vanished. Seems to me like your prison is broken." the queen said sternly. "If you've been here all this time, what," the queen wanted to pass her frustration and hurt upon the dragon, "what were you doing? Why not come out and help me fight? To convince everyone, that I'm not insane?"

"Unfortunately, your highness, we all have our burdens. And yours is not one I can lift off your shoulders. As to the reason why I stay here, is to avoid war." said the dragon.

"War? War with whom?" asked Erlen.

"War with your kind. All it takes is for your kind to see me, and they will get scared. Then they will want to kill what they fear. All it takes is for one lunatic to rise and stir the rest of your kingdom, to hunt me down. And if you are not with them, then you are against them. And if against them, then your head they will have." unfiltered the dragon.

"My people are not like that? They would never," the queen was interrupted.

"Before you speak for you people, speak to the other dead descendants scattered across your oceans. Tell it to their people who took it not seriously that they held something of great value on their back. Tell it to my kind, hunted, and killed. And of course, your husband and his men, can you say the same about them?" stroke the dragon.

Unable to respond, the queen stayed silent. Being not one for small talks the dragon spoke. "Why are you here, your highness? What is it you want from me?" Not waiting for her answer, the dragon lid ablaze a full circle around them. Trapping both it and the queen at the center. Now it was entirely visible to the queen. It was bigger than she imagined. Its size was something to be fearful of. Its jaws and mouth were big enough to swallow three men simultaneously. Repeating its question, it said, "now, your highness, what is it you want from me?"

Before the queen could answer, a faint, yet clear shriek like scream reached the dragon's ears.

"What? What is it?" asked Erlen, as she looked around to see if she could catch wind of what the dragon was sensing.

"It sounded like a call," said the dragon.

"Is that good or bad?" asked Erlen.

"It depends on whom it was intended for." replied the dragon. Its returned focus on the queen was cut short, as a familiar sound reached its ears. It was recognizable as if it were heard yesterday. "NO, IT CAN'T BE.," said the dragon.

"What can't be? What did you hear?" asked Erlen impatiently and wanting to know what was happening outside.

"It's him," said the dragon.

"Him who? You're not making much sense, you know that?" said an irritated queen.

"It's Tish!" Yelled the dragon. "He can't be, he can't be free. We sealed him in that barrier centuries ago."

"Um, I guess you miss the part where I told you, your prison wasn't a prison anymore, huh." yelled back the queen. "Who is this Tish?"

"Tish is not one you can mess with. If your kind killed my kind across that ocean, Tish is not one, they can defeat. It took seven of us to fight him. How much of my kind you think are left alive?" asked the dragon.

"They can't all be dead. I am pretty sure they are alive somewhere. Hiding just like you." answered Erlen.

"They are all gone. Not one is left alive. And without their help, we can't win against him." said the dragon.

"I refuse to give up. Here you were, sound asleep not a care in the world, and you want me to give up hope? No, I will not. I've got allies across the border and he will help me." revealed Erlen.

"He? I do not know whom you are talking about, but the person that can be of use to us at the moment is the conqueror. If he is around, we have a fighting chance. Where is your general?"

"My general? My general is out taking over my kingdom and limiting my authority as we speak. There's no way, I'm going to ask him for help." replied Erlen.

"He's not talking about Vasquez your highness," startling them both was a figure that laid in wait in the shadows. "He's talking about the king of Serdio. Bervard and his brother Philip."

"Adasa? Is that you?" asked Erlen, surprised.

"It is I, your highness. Where you go, we go. You are our body, and we are your shadow." said Adasa approaching forward, toward the light of the flames and along with her three others, surrounding the dragon.

"Oh!" marveled the dragon, "there is yet hope for us. The clan of Shadows! And to think I had thought you guys were extinct. If you live, then surely so are your masters. Where are they?" asked the dragon.

"Our masters are gone. We failed the first, and the second flew away to a place we know not," replied Adasa.

"So, one like me may yet still live," said the dragon with a sign of hope.

Queen Erlen began to feel light-headed again. Not only were her spies not scared of the dragon, but they knew of the existence of his kind entirely. She needed to know more. She wanted to know more.

"Allow me to explain my queen." Said Hadi, another among the four, before the queen could ask.

CHAPTER 13

Brief History

"We're from the clan of shadows. We hunt and live in the shadows. As you are already aware. We can infiltrate anywhere. As per your request once, even within the castle of Serdio. That of course having been caught by Sirius. He, like us, is the same. We, those before us, served your kind. A guardian and key keeper like yourself. And together with a dragon at our side, we ruled our lands. Everything was peaceful, it was said. Until creed and power ravaged our land. The army who should have protected their king killed him instead. We who were supposed to protect him from all danger, we, who were supposed to know every enemy before they became an enemy, failed to protect him." said Hadi as the queen and dragon listened.

"Viz was our dragon. She was our king's dragon. She trained us in the art of concealment. Due to our failure to protect the king, she left us to fend for ourselves. Being not much of fighters ourselves, it was a massacre. Our ancestors saw it best to come here, where it all began, for refuge. Your great, great grandfather feared us outsiders and raged war against us. Your general at that time, from the clan of conquerors, saw us as fit to hunt, for our abilities. It took your great grandfather to offer us lenience and put an end to our extinction. Your young king at that time caused a rift between his desires and his late father's general. With one wanting our survival, and the other our heads." said Adasa.

Hadi continued, "That's when the kingdom became two. With plenty of unknown creatures in the land, the commander was busy enjoying himself. That is until there was nothing left to conquer."

"That's when war broke out," said Adasa.

"We won of course because we were more in numbers. However, a few of us after the war joined side with the commander in anger of what Viz had done to them, once they find out of the existence of Alshbar," said Hadi.

"Alshbar?" questioned queen Erlen.

"Alshbar, the dragon before you," said Adasa.

"So, you do have a name. I guess that should have been my first question to you, huh," said Erlen. "What happened afterward?"

"To cut the history short. A second war broke out and Henri, that was what they called themselves, still lost. This time, Alshbar helped. And as punishment, all of our kind that had joined the general was executed, and they were blamed for losing the war." continued Hadi.

"That can't be right. You said Serdio, had one just like you. One from your clan. Surely one of them survived?" said Erlen.

"That's correct. A child survived and grew. Our ancestors before us, trained every descendant of that child. Just as we have trained Sirius. But Sirius, unlike his predecessor, is faithful to his crown. And thus, not an ally to us." revealed Hadi.

"Before you say a word your highness, yes we are dangerous. But you need not worry. Our ancestors failed in the past; we will not do the same. We have eyes and ears everywhere. What happened to our first king will never be repeated in history. We swore our allegiance to your great grandfather and the crown. As far as we are concerned, you are the crown. Not the king." said Adasa.

"And Sirius?" asked Erlen.

"Sirius is not an enemy nor an ally. But if there is ever a need for collaboration, he will be one we can count on," revealed Adasa.

"Why was I not told of any of this? Why is there no mention of this in the kingdom's records?" asked Erlen.

"Your highness, the number of people that have access to these records are too great to restrict. Thus, why we keep our records. Away from prying eyes. And, unfortunately from you too, my queen." said Hadi.

"Why? What have I ever done to you to keep this from me?" asked Erlen.

"Nothing your highness," said Adasa, quickly kneeling before her highness.

"Then why?" sobbed Erlen.

"It is because of the king. The king and his general and commanders. If they had ever found out what we revealed to you, he would want to use us to start another war. And as things stand, Henri is much stronger than we are. King Bervard, would welcome the idea of war and would stop at nothing to conquer this land and take the lives of the royals of this land. The king, we care little for, but you and especially now that you have a child, we couldn't run the risk." said Adasa.

"And the dragon? Alsh…, whatever your name is," said Erlen as she wiped tears from her cheeks.

"We didn't know about him." Said Hadi. "We followed you here and only stumbled upon his existence when he dragged you out of the room. Our records make no mention of what happened to him. Most likely because of the desertion of our kind that happened."

Regaining her composure, queen Erlen asked, "so, what now?" Looking at Alshbar.

"Your Highness, I am afraid I can't be much of assistance to you. You have yet to tell me what it is you want from me." Said Alshbar.

"My queen, before you speak, I think it is important to listen to what we have to say." Said Saiji approaching forward.

"Speak." Ordered the queen as she regained the composure worthy of a ruler.

"We surveyed the land as you requested but found nothing in connection or evidence of an outbreak. As we speak, we have three of our kind missing. They were sent to patrol the surrounding area around the dark forest. We have sent reinforcement and currently are waiting for their return. Concerning the commander, he is nowhere to be found.

My best guess would be the dark forest, where..." Saiji was interrupted.

"Why there? I thought no one could enter that place?" Asked the queen.

"No, that's not true. Only those with good hearts can freely enter and come out. If your general is evil as I have come to hear from his lips, then there's no way he can enter." Said Alshbar.

"That's not all." Continued Saiji. "As to whether he is in the dark forest or not, what lies near it is equally important. Soldiers and monsters alike made camp there. Our best guess would be that the commander is staging a coup. Of course, we cannot confirm this. But it does not look like the commander fulfilled his duties in eradicating the land of those monsters. It seems your Highness, and I say this with sad news, that villagers have been used as food for his new army. We found a mass grave behind the dark forest, near Henrian territory." Informed Saiji.

"Why am I now learning this?" Asked Erlen in anger.

"It took us a while to gather this information. We lost 19 of our comrades. 19." Yelled Adasa.

"Adasa, don't." Begged Hadi.

"No, she needs to stop acting like a child! You are a queen. The world will not like you! And if they do, then tomorrow they will hate you. So, what does it matter if your husband thinks you are crazy? So, what your authority has been dulled around the general and commanders you remain a queen. So, for once, swallow up your feeling shove them down. Because if you think governing is all that simple, you're wrong!" Yelled Adasa at the queen as she approached closer and closer.

"Adasa, you went too far." Admitted Saiji, kneeling before the queen asking for her forgiveness.

"No, Adasa is right. Our lives are at stake. Our mission. The crown and the world. Your Highness, if you cannot grasp the situation, then I recommend you let us take over. Though our method would be less conventional, it'll unite both kingdoms and put an end to this threat." Spoke the last of the spies, Sòna.

"What, assassinate the Royals of Henri and force them to serve our cause?" Questioned Erlen.

"Something like that." Boldly replied Sòna.

"As if that'll ever work." Retorted the queen.

"We don't want history to be repeated. Your safety is our priority. Yours and that of the other two like you... Ay, you, weren't supposed to know that yet." Said Hadi, regretting that she spoke.

Erlen was puzzled as was Alshbar. "Alshbar said they were all dead. Wha, what are you saying?" Erlen was getting emotional. "Am I not your queen?"

"Yes." They all answered in unison.

"Then why treat me like everybody else?" Asked Erlen.

"Because that is how you treat yourself." Bluntly replied Adasa. Her response caused the other three spies to cast angry looks at her.

"My queen. The reason we did not tell was because of your husband. Everything you know, you desperately want him to know as well. You desperately seek from him something which he cares not to provide. And your enemies, mainly the general knows this. All it takes is a bit of ale and wine and everything you told him in secret he spills out. We couldn't risk it." Revealed Sòna.

"And telling you to not talk to him, would be torture for you. Am I wrong?" Cautiously asked Hadi.

Withholding her tears Erlen mumbled under her breath, "I never asked for any of this." Raising her voice, she addressed Saiji. "What about Philip, where is he now?"

"The last report we received said they were still in the whispering forest. They'd captured a creature that runs incredibly fast."

"Fast you say. If memory serves correctly, they are the type you want to deal with quickly. They are both scouts and seekers. The worst to have to sneak up on you on the Battlefield." Said Alshbar. "That explains what I heard earlier. It was used to spy on Henri. Based on your spies, the king of Henri is the conqueror I am looking for. If that is the case, it is no wonder Tish wants to go after him. I must go to him at once."

"STOP!" Yelled Erlen. Just stop. For once and let me rule. Taking in a deep breath, she spoke, "Saiji, how far is Philip from us?"

"Assuming that he is still in the forest, I'd say a day's ride."
Answered Saiji. "Why?"

"You mentioned an army near the dark forest. Are all the
commanders accounted for?" Asked Erlen.

"Yes, they are all with the king." Answered Adasa. "What
are you planning your Highness?"

"What are our numbers inside the castle?" Asked Erlen.

"We have around eight hundred able men, your Highness."
Answered Hadi.

Pacing back and forth, queen Erlen was thinking of the best
outcome for her limited resources.

"Saiji, how many more of your sisters were sent to
investigate the surrounding dark forest?" Asked the queen.

"On top of the nineteen comrades, we lost I sent an
additional twelve. Six to track the whereabouts of general
Vasquez. The other six to further investigate the
disappearance of the villagers." Replied Saiji.

Before Erlen could ask when the next report would come
in, a voice interrupted from the shadows. "I pardon for the
intrusion. A report just came in." The clan of shadows was
well organized. You never saw them coming or leaving.
They could relay a message faster than a bird. With their
handmade bows, their custom arrows could travel great
distances. And that is how the information got around.
When on a mission, they knew exactly how many were
needed to relay messages depending on distance alone.

Approaching Sòna, the newcomer handed her the parchment that was attached to the arrow. Unrolling it, Sòna said, "dragon, I need more light." Taking no offense, Alshbar lit his dying ring of fire once more. With better light, Sòna began to read.

'We must evacuate the queen and her daughter immediately. General is coming to kill her. To destroy her seal to the barrier. Sirius is among us. He needs help. Currently causing chaos in the enemy camp. Send word out to Henri. Dragon has its sight on King Bervard. His ability to rally people to his cause is something they fear. If we lose here, the world crumbles. If we lose here, there will be no one left to seek help from across the ocean.' "end of the message." Said Sòna, looking up at the queen as she awaited further orders.

"Your Highness, what is it you want from me?" Stressed Alshbar.

Pacing back and forth she laid out her situation in her head. 'two enemies on two fronts. One we can hold off. The other is too strong. If Henri manages to take care of that dragon, then in two days tops, we could expect help from king Brevard. Or rather Philip. They have got their three hundred men; their castle will not fall so easily. I have got my spies, so the information will not be much of a problem. I have a dragon that can help me on both fronts. But which is best to start with.' questioned her, as she looked at Alshbar.

As if reading her thoughts, Alshbar spoke. "If you are worried about the king, fear not, I have a seer. Years ago, a young man, tried to come through that entrance. A merchant, I think he was. He saw me in his visions he said.

Visions he kept having every night. Ironclad was his name. I will try to reach out to him. Though it has been years since we last spoke." Said Alshbar.

"Good you do that." Said the queen. "If we did not know of your existence, then certainty, neither do they. Alshbar, I need you to rescue Sirius and what remains of my spies. Can you do that?" Erlen asked.

"Your orders are all, I've been waiting for." Said Alshbar.

"One more thing," added Erlen, "once you've rescued him, head towards king Bervard. It is risky. But if you manage to contact this Ironclad of yours, judging by my experience, seeing is believing." Nodding, Alshbar took off in the shadows of the cave.

"What about us, your Highness?" Asked Saiji.

"It is safe to assume that the general wouldn't have staged a coup if he weren't gaining aid from within the Castle's walls. Gather your forces. I need everyone inside these walls within the hour." Ordered the queen.

"Consider it done." Replied Saiji, as she disappeared into the shadow of the cave. To later being seen running through the room of records toward the stairs.

"As for you Sòna," Erlen paused, "thank you!" Bowing down before her queen, Sòna and the others were proud to see her in action. "Now," Erlen continued, "I need for the commanders and king to be sobered up. You have my one-time permission to roughen them up." Smirk the queen.

"With pleasure!" Replied and enthusiastic Sòna.

"You come with me!" Ordered Sòna of the messenger.

"Adasa, Hadi. Your duties won't be so pleasant." Warned the queen.

"Worry not, our queen. Just give us your orders." They replied together.

"Take as many spies as you need. Change into plain clothes and fish out every spy working for the general. Every out of place soldier. Fully awake and anxious. If they react violently to you roaming about, then more likely they are with the Vasquez. Take them out. We want little to no opening when the enemy gets here. I want a complete sweep of the castle and surrounding villages. None is too high for your assassination blades. Safe the king and commanders. Those you lock up in a cell if found guilty. We will figure out what to do with them once the storm passes. You have half an hour to do this. And the other half to clean up. Leave no traces. We do not want to alarm our dear general Vasquez. If we do this right, by tonight, I'll have served to our enemies the same humiliation they inflicted upon me."

"We're on it." Adasa and Hadi responded in unison.

"As for me, once all is set, I'll sound the bells of war." Said queen Erlen as she walked back to her chambers.

CHAPTER 14

Celebration or Funeral?

Two days early, walking down the corridor of the castle of Henri, early in the morning, a beautiful Kathryn was all smiles.

"What's got you smiling so bright Kathryn?" asked Miriam.

"Your highness, I didn't notice you. How rude of me." Taking a bow, she greeted the queen.

"How is your son? Is he healing well?" asked the queen.

"I fear he is healing too quickly your highness. Darrius already wants to go on another adventure with Marcus. Can you imagine that? As if facing off against seven wolves for two twelve years old's could be called an adventure." Complained Kathryn.

"Let's not talk about that this early in the morning," said Miriam in a somewhat sarcastic voice. "At least your husband won't spare your son from a spanking. Mine's will boast about Marcus' achievements to the whole village," said Miriam, to which they both laughed.

"But, though dangerous and reckless they were yesterday, they did save the baker's daughter. We can't hold it against them. They are their father's son, alright." said Kathryn, as she turned around to leave.

"Uh, uh, not so fast." said Miriam, "you still have not answered my previous question. "Why are you all smiles this morning?"

Turning around to face the queen, Kathryn was blushing. "I got a letter from Philip yesterday. He said their mission throughout the land was coming to an end and that he'll be here soon in the coming days."

"Well, that's great news! That must mean Bervard will soon be here as well. It has been too long," Miriam sighed. "I want to be held in his arms as he tells me of all his feats. I must prepare for his coming. It has been four lonely months without my husband. I intend to make the most of his first night back if you know what I mean!" said Miriam as she winked at a blushing Kathryn. Clapping her hands, she gestured for the royal maids. "My husband will be coming soon, my skin needs to be silky smooth. Prepare me a bath."

Looking back, Kathryn was head down lost in thoughts. "What are you waiting for Kathryn, your skin won't get soft by itself you know. Chop, chop, you too need to prepare."

Mumbling, Kathryn, couldn't verbally decline Miriam's invitation.

Getting a bit annoyed, Miriam asked, "what is it? What aren't you telling me?"

Timidly speaking up, Kathryn said, "Philip asked that I join him at the cabin. On his way back he'll stop there first."

"You are so lucky!" exclaimed a giggling queen. "You had your plans all along didn't you? I see now that I wasn't the only one who could not bear these four months of solitude." Retreating from Kathryn, Miriam yelled out, "four months of unmet desires!"

Embarrass, Kathryn ran through the hall, away from Miriam. She couldn't hide her joy of wanting to see her husband. It had indeed been months of solitude. But most importantly of worrying. Worrying about whether the king would do something foolish that would endanger, his brother, her husband, Philip's life. But now that they are well, and that he had asked her to meet him at their cabin, meant he had lots to tell her. Lot's he wanted to get off his chest and hear her words of comfort. Oh, she too longed to be in the arms of her husband and once again be able to gaze at his calm demeanor as he sleeps. To have him around on the constant and hear him call her beautiful. To hear him say, "you are far too beautiful for me. Throughout the world, there is only you. None equals your beauty." How she longed for those words, as he ran his hand through her hair. "Soon! Very soon, we shall be together again!" Kathryn said to herself in excitement and smiles as she headed down the castle interiors, in preparation for her departure.

Making her way to the stable, she asked that her carriage be made ready. Heading back to her chambers, she packed the necessities for the cabin. Calling her maidens, she instructed them to take it all to her carriage. So full of excitement was Kathryn, that she forgot about Darrius. A Darrius who so happened to be walking through her door, arms, and legs wrapped up in blood spotted bandages. Holding in his hands a paper, he wasted no time in settling down in his mother's presence, and began to read out loud,

"Oh my sweet Kathryn,

It is with great joy and anticipation that I get to write to you, to inform you of the closure of our quest. The monsters that once plagued our people are no more. Peace once again reigns. Though it may be temporary, I long to spend the little time it may last in your presence. To have your sweet scent upon me once more. To hold you in my arms, and hear you ease my worries and concerns away. Yes, my dove, I long for your presence, as nature yearns for Spring during the winter. Come forth and meet me at our cabin. I shall instruct that we rest before entering triumphantly back home so that we can have the whole night to us. My beautiful dove."

Kathryn was too embarrassed to stop Darrius who was now surrounded by the maidens, as they took in every word. Having finished reading his father's letter, Darrius looked up at his mother and asked, "does that mean that I'm going to have a little brother?" The maids present could not help holding back their laughter as they rushed to Kathryn who had hidden her face in the palms of her hands. Teasing her, but yet putting her at ease, they exited her chambers, leaving just her and Darrius.

Walking toward Darrius with a bright red face of joy, she knelt before him. "Darrius, that letter wasn't addressed to you. That was not yours to read. Let alone, out loud. Why do you have that in your hands' son?" asked Kathryn.

"I got it from your bed. I heard you running in the corridor. And the only thing that gets you that excited is seeing dad back. So I went to your window to see the courtyard, but there was no one there. That's when I saw it on your bed."

revealed Darrius. "Does that mean I'm going to have a little brother?"

A bit annoyed that her son read her letter out loud and that he read it at all, she couldn't bring herself to punish his innocence. "Why do you keep on asking that? Who put that idea in your head?" Kathryn got curious. "Wait, if you grab the letter from my bed, why'd you come into my room with it? Darrius, who else read your dad's letter?"

Realizing his mother wasn't going to like the answer to that question. Darrius started retreating, taking big steps backward. Shooting a stern look of reprisal at her son, Kathryn advanced toward him. "Darrius?"

"Ok, ok, but promise me I can come with you. I want to tell dad of the wolves Marcus and I fought off," asked Darrius.

"Young man, you are in no position to bargain with me. So, choose now, either I have Irwin watch over you while I am gone, or you stay here with Marcus. Which do you choose?" asked Kathryn, outsmarting her son.

"I'm stuck here either way." retorted Darrius.

"I see. I guess I can go ahead and ask Irwin to watch you then in my absence," said Kathryn, intimidating her son to talk.

"No mom, please! Captain Irwin is a stiff rock, he does nothing fun. Will not even let me go to the toilet until it is break time. No, anything but Irwin." begged Darrius.

"Ah, so Marcus it shall be then. So, who else read my letter?" asked Kathryn a second time.

"Well...," paused Darrius, "I chased you down the hallway, but couldn't find you. I saw auntie Miriam and asked her if she saw you. That is when she grabbed the letter from my hands. She laughed and told me, 'looks like you may have a little brother soon.' That's it, just her, I swear."

Grabbing Darrius by his scarred shoulders, looking full of embarrassment Kathryn said, "I need to get out of here."

"What about me?" asked Darrius wincing from the pain.

"As for you young man," said Kathryn as she headed out the door, "you get to stay here, and think about what you've done." Taking a good look at her son, she said, "really, of all people she had to read it. I won't ever hear the end of it. Miriam will tease me for life."

"Mom, it's just a letter." replied an irritated Darrius.

"Oh, you'll see when you're married. Oh, you can count on it. It is not just a letter." Approaching her son halfway and calling him to do the same, she continued, "it's not just a letter, it's intimate. It is personal, it is sacred. And one day when you get older, you'll understand." She said in sweetness as she ran her hand through Darrius' hair.

"Yuck, I won't be writing letters when I'm older, I can tell you that. I shall be on the battlefield not writing letters to girls and asking them to meet me. Real men don't do that." Darrius said with pride.

"Oh yeah!? What do real men do then?" asked Kathryn smiling.

"Well, they do what dad and uncle do. They go fight monsters and wars and come back and tell of their adventures. They drink and fight and train and fart naked in the morning." giggled Darrius.

"Oh wow. I was so wrong." giggled back Kathryn. "I see you know what a real man is then," said she as she kissed his forehead. "Now, concerning this letter, there are things in there that I'll, or rather your dad will explain to you when you're older."

"Nah, I'll pass. I won't have time for that." said a prideful Darius with two hands on his hips.

"Darrius? Did you read the back of this letter?" asked a puzzled Kathryn.

"What? There was more? What does it say?" responded a curious Darius.

Blushing and relieved, Kathryn patted Darius. on the head and said, "you're right, you don't have time for love letters." Laughing uncontrollably at the thought of embarrassment, she exited her chambers right after saying her goodbyes to Darius.

"Oh, if you think I'm going to stay here, you are dead wolf butt wrong mother," mumbled Darius to himself.

Having earlier asked the maids to prepare and pack her wagon with what she would need, Kathryn was ready to go. The air is fresh, with dew still visible through the sun's rays, it was a beautiful morning. Being accompanied by ten guards and two maidservants, Miriam set out on her adventure and destination.

Meanwhile, in the castle, Marcus woke up with sores and scars. He had more scars than Darrius. Having in the end being the only one conscious, he fought off the remaining wolves to protect an unconscious Darrius and the baker's daughter. Out of the three, the baker's daughter was the worst. The state at which her mulled leg was found, Marcus wondered if it would be cut off.

Posturing himself to sit up from his bed, he did so in pain. "Young master, you shouldn't try to move. Your wounds have yet to close." said the maid keeping watch on him.

"I'll be alright. I want to go see Darrius. Can you help me?" asked the young prince.

"First things first, I need to dress your wounds with fresh bandages," said the maid as she did just that. By the time she was finished, Kathryn was long gone.

Getting up to leave his room, Marcus opened his bedroom door to find his mother standing in front of it. "And where do you think you're going in that state of yours?" asked Miriam.

"Mom," "your, highness," both Marcus and the maid responded. "I was going to check on Darrius, I swear," responded Marcus.

"Darrius is in far better shape than you, I can tell you that." Said Miriam coldly. "You could have gotten yourself killed and now you refuse to stay in bed and heal. What am I to do with you," said Miriam.

"Mom, I'm alright, I am safe. We are all safe," replied Marcus.

"Yeah, now you are. What if that was not the case? What if you had died? What would I have told your father then?" asked Miriam.

"Well, that's easy," joked Marcus, "you'd tell him I fought off wolves and saved lives."

Lightly smacking her son behind the head, Miriam responded, "you idiot, if you had died, so would have Darrius and the girl. And besides, if Captain Irwin had not found you in time, who knows what would have happened."

"Mom, I'm fine. It is the baker's daughter you should be worried about. How is she?" asked Marcus.

Looking at her son, she could not help but see her husband in him. But not totally. Marcus was Marcus. Bold like his dad, courageous, a fighter, a winner, and conqueror. Yet, his love for violence bends toward protection rather than glory. Exactly like his uncle. Though Philip, fears losing lives altogether, Marcus puts he's on the line to save others. "So young and so foolish," mumbled Miriam. And before Marcus could ask what she had spoken, she answered his previous question, "she is well as far as I've been told. But she may never be able to walk normally on that leg of hers." informed Miriam.

"Can I go see her, after I see Darrius?" asked Marcus insistently.

"You are in no position to travel, besides, she's in the village with her mother," answered Miriam. Knowing her son would ask why she was not being treated in the castle, she continued, "they don't have enough money to afford the necessary treatment."

Giving her mother a stern, angry and detesting look, "why must they have money? Can we not provide it to them? Were the wounds and scars that I've gotten in vain?" asked Marcus.

"Young man, your actions were payment enough. If you did die, and she had lived, no amount of money would be enough for your heroic foolish act," replied Miriam with a mother's anger.

"If I did die, which I didn't, and she lived, which she did, at least, at least," Marcus could not bring himself to utter what he was thinking. *"At least I'd have saved a life and not allowed another family to mourn a child, unlike dad and his quests for glory."*

"At least what?" pushed Miriam. "At least you saved a life. Sure. And in return leave this kingdom without an heir. Is that what you want? To die early chasing fame and glory?"

Lowering his head in defeat, Marcus responded, "I couldn't care less for fame or glory. Others chase after them, and it won't be me." Marcus' defeat was in realizing his mom was right. If he had died, there would be no heir to replace his dad if he ever did fall in his current quest. *"Idiot,"* he said to himself. Walking toward his bed, he turned his back to Miriam as he laid down to rest.

Queen Miriam stayed staring at her son's back. She could not bear the thoughts of losing her only child. The only child to be birthed by her and the king. "You're not replaceable Marcus, you're our only child. My only child, if you die, I die. If you want to save your future subject, I best recommend that you learn what leadership is. And" Marcus could hear his mother's footsteps getting closer, "the hearts of your subjects. Not everyone, deserves you bleeding on their behalf. Do remember that."

Sitting on her son's bed, Miriam ordered the maid to leave the room. Continuing her lecture, "your father's way of life, give his men reasons to train, to be strong, to chase after glory versus cowering before danger. That way of his, brought about the extinction of wild beasts and creatures, that would not even have allowed you to step outside the castle's doors. That is his way of life, his way of leading. Think now on what you want your reign to be," said Miriam as she stroked her son's hair. "I am proud of you, you know. You and Darrius, you both are something else you know that" said Miriam as she smiled. *"Ten years barren, I can't lose you,"* reflected Miriam on her deepest hurt and fear.

Rolling over, Marcus gazed upon the tears in his mother's eyes. Placing his hand over hers, he said, "I'll be smarter, mom. I'll do better." Kissing her son's forehead, Miriam got up to leave. "I love you son."

Pacing toward the door, a knock was heard. Opening it, one of Kathryn's maids was standing there. "Your highness, good morning" greeted the maid.

"Fair morning to you. What is it that you need?" asked the queen.

"Lady Kathryn asked that I watched over Darrius in her absence. I can't find him anywhere, so I wondered if by any chance he could be with the young prince." asked the maid.

Placing her hand over her belly, queen Miriam laughed happily. "I see I'm not the only one with my hands full."

"Your highness?" the maid was puzzled.

"Darrius is not here. If you cannot find him in the castle, then it is safe to assume that he is long gone. Oh, I wish I could be there to see your reaction when you find out you have an extra passenger Kathryn." said Miriam as she closed the door behind her, leaving Marcus to rest.

"Why do you always leave me alone by myself Darrius?" said Marcus in the silence of his room.

With the queen now gone, the maid that was attending Marcus, came back in. Marcus looking up at her pondered hard at what he wanted to do. Hesitating for a bit, he said, "I need you to do something for me."

"What is it your highness?" asked the maid.

"It concerns Cateline, the baker's daughter." said the Prince.

CHAPTER 15

Alshbar, a Friend

As the king and company were retreating from the forest, and the atmosphere still smelled of regrets and mistrust, something came crashing in the forest, sending smoke and dirt up in the night's sky. Whereas all the soldiers at camp heard it, they only pursued once they saw King Bervard doing so. And those that were near it, feared their doom had come.

"Robert! Robert, where are you?" called out a frantic general.

"I'm over here," replied Robert coughing. Robert could not understand why Black still had his back turned toward the threat that entered their presence. *"Did he betray us?"* thought Robert. Faintly making out a shape among the smoke, the creature, or so it seemed rose in heights of fifty to sixty feet. Wasting no time to establish dominance, the newcomer went about producing the same sound and call that they had previously heard after Nek sent out his location. However, the only difference was that they were seeing spewing flames. "Black, what did you do?" questioned Robert.

Flapping its wings to spread off the smoke, Alshbar came into view. And when the rest of the camp led by the king entered the forest with torches, it was fully visible. The dragon was grayish. Moving about in full circle looking at all those who surrounded him, Alshbar examined the courage of each one. Having landed his eyes on the king, he said, "The conquering King. It is an honor to finally meet you in person," thus shocking everyone.

Taking back, by its politeness, but more so, by the fact that it could speak, the king was not sure what to do. But that did not surprise Black's close companions. They believed him without a doubt, and it showed. There was a certain pride and joy on Black's face as he stared at his fellow lieutenants. Not one of them showed signs of remorse or disbelief.

Looking at Black, John said "Black?"

Black knew exactly what John was asking and responded, "you can trust him."

Hesitantly but surely, the lieutenants put their weapons away and got closer to observe what laid before them. Philip was too stupefied to move and so was the king, but more so because a legendary creature greeted the king.

"Ironclad, gather the crown and your most loyal men, we don't have much time," said Alshbar as it left their presence and headed deeper into the forest.

Words cannot describe the faces of the rest of the soldiers. Even if the king were to charge into battle, none would follow. This, the thing they were seeing before them, they were having a hard time registering. "General," called out Black, "what do we do now?"

Trying to gain his senses all the while clearing his throat, Philip responded slowly, "the. The plan is the same. We are to lift camp. Only the essentials are to be taken." Philip cleared his throat. "No torches are to be lid tonight as we retreat. And uh, um, the king and I, um, we will uh, go talk to your dragon friend over there. Um, Bervard, the sooner we hear what it has to say the faster we can leave this forest."

Sensing their general's fear, the lieutenants replied, one after the other. "General, are you sure you want to do that? I mean what if it lures you and the king to eat you guys," said John scarily.

"That's right sir," said Smith, "how do we know what it is, to begin with. What if it is not even a dragon. What if it wants to take our forms so that it can become us?" Said Smith, sending chills down Philip's spine.

"Even worse, what if it was sent by the kingdom of Serdio to trick us into lowering our guard?" said Robert.

The king understanding what was going on whispered to Philip, "you know, they may be right. And since I am the king, I cannot die here. I too sense that it is a trick. If it decides to eat us, I want you to force your way down its throat and kill it from within. Can you do that brother?"

Philip was dumbfounded. This was too big of an event for him to properly think straight. All that kept going in his mind was being eaten by a talking beast. A talking beast! As if the size of its teeth and claws were not enough. The creature could talk.

"Oh, come on! Of all the scenarios I ever imagined, this was one I never imagined you being incapable of handling." Said Malvin. "General, they are all messing with you."

"They're what?" Philip was puzzled. Turning around to face his subjects and king, he found them all laughing. "Wait, are you kidding me right now? Oh! How could I have let you do this to me? You guys are, so, getting punished for this." Philip was back to his senses. At which point the lieutenants could no longer hold their laughter silent.

"And do what?" questioned a hysterical Smith, "have us eating to death, by a giant talking bird?"

"Wait, those exist?" questioned Philip forgetting his anger. In their laughter, the lieutenants left Philip behind and walked toward the dragon, laughing all the more at his question.

"Oh, dear brother, who would have thought that I would have such a story to tell my son and grand-kids. This is priceless. This must be written in our history. The day the great General Philip froze before a talking dragon." Smiling himself, king Bervard patted his brother on the shoulder as he left him standing alone.

"What, what did I do?" Philip was puzzled.

"That's exactly it commander. It is your face. That was priceless." replied Malvin, as he too, left and headed toward the others.

Not understanding what that was about, Philip followed them. The lieutenants went and confidently joined Black who was in extreme proximity with the dragon. The king and general kept their distance out of precaution. Malvin and Edwin wanted to join, but out of respect to rank, they kept their distance.

"Good, you are all here. We do not have much time. The survival of the lives on this land and distant ones is at stake. I need you to listen very closely. This is my task for you guys. Accomplish it and we may have a fighting chance." Said Alshbar, skipping the introductions.

No one talked. No one dared to. "Sirius is making his way toward Serdio as we speak. He is to infiltrate the castle and protect the royals. King Bervard, due to the number of enemies they will be facing, they will not last long. Many lives will be lost, but it cannot be helped. The royals are your top priorities. General, I need you to go back to your castle. Assemble your forces. You are at war. The enemy of your neighbor is now your enemy. You must not let them down. As for Tish, I will slow him down. I've done it before and I'll do it again, even if it'll be the last thing I do after these many years of slumber." Ordered the dragon.

King Bervard was having none of it. "You must not know on whose land you stand. This is the kingdom of Henri. We do not take orders from outsiders. Much less from those who played dead. We give the orders. I give orders to the men you see before you. None other." said the king of Henri in pride and anger. "If Serdio needs saving, then they'll send an official request for help with conditions of relinquishing all rights to their territory. That is how I do things. Their king has not been much help in keeping his men and his side of the border chaos-free. We have had our shares of bloodshed on our lands and they were not by our hands. Villages had been burnt, orphans we had to raise. Men, we have had to execute for their failure of securing the border. My men. If they need help, they may as well go find it at the bottom of a well."

"This is going to be troublesome," Malvin whispered.

To which Bervard heard and responded in kind. "Indeed, it will be. Serdio can fall as far as I'm concerned. You of all people should agree with me, captain. Or is it that you forgot the bandits that killed your parents were from Serdio?" Bervard had touched a nerve.

Immediately Malvin's demeanor changed. Pulling out his sword he charged at Bervard. The king, not a bit shocked nor taken off guard, pulled out his sword. And just like that, blade met blade and blades broke blades. Both swords laid in ruin, in pieces on the floor. Before the king and Malvin struck swords, Robert was quickly restrained by John and Smith. Robert, a hand on his sword, was unable to make a single move. His comrades had him pinned down. "Wait it out, Robert. Let them settle their differences." John told him. "You know my bow's fast. None of them will die tonight. You have my word." reassured Smith.

"Oh, believe me, your highness, I have not forgotten anything. I remember clearly those responsible were your men as you mentioned. Had they done their job; my parents would still be alive. Serdio is not the only guilty one in this. Both nations are responsible. The common people are not to pay for the sins of their rulers. If you are so great of a king as you say you are, the least you could do is win the hearts of the innocent in Serdio and offer them shelter. That is what a great king would do, your highness." Sarcasm Malvin.

"Boy don't test my rule. You are way too young to be my judge. Where were you when exotic creatures feasted on my people? Where were you when my father the king, asked Serdio for help and they wished him dead along with our people? Where were you when skirmishes broke out on the border and lives were lost? The only reason why you still live is because your lieutenants are still useful to me as a soldier. Once he becomes of no use, my restraint for you will be lifted as well as that of Robert. You're a good captain BUT FALL IN LINE!" Yelled the king as both he and Malvin butted heads.

Philip who did not say a word, nor move, was calculating the best course of action. Having found it, he offered his advice. "My king, if I may, it would be in our advantage to take over Serdio as it stands. Make use of the chaos. Save and occupy it. Perfect chance to dethrone your foe and reunite the land."

"Nice try Philip. But I will not be moving. We were weak in the past. But now, we can hold our own, against them. And let us not forget, what was it that killed our great, great king. This very dragon you see before you. You do remember the story, don't you brother?" asked Bervard, shocking everyone else listening.

"No need to doubt my memory. I carry that history with me every day. But far be it from me to rule with injustice as our forefathers did. As Malvin said, you cannot guilt your enemy without incriminating yourself. We too have bloodshed on our hands. Blood for blood. Village for village. Livestock for livestock. As the king that Silas is, would you not be disappointed if he did not live up to your expectations?" Asked Philip.

Bervard did not answer. Philip continued, "if you won't do it for Silas and Erlen than do it for the dead infants we killed with our hands. For the mothers and fathers whose children we stripped them of." At those words, Bervard's body jerk, as one remembering a nightmare. Back then, Bervard was a young prince. A group of villagers from Serdio sought refuge in Henri, running away from famine and bandits. Bandits, that were in fact mercenaries causing chaos in both countries in hopes that war would break out. Henrian soldiers at the time, acting on their own, took it upon themselves to avenge their people. In wanting to inflict the greatest of pain for what was thought to be an invasion and killings done by Serdio, the soldiers slaughtered the young Serdians. Boys and girls, as their parents watch their sufferings. By the time the castle was made aware of this, nearly the entire refugees were annihilated. And those who were alive, were not for long, due to the torture inflicted on them.

"Aye. For them, yes. I'll reunite this land, and will judge all those still alive, that are responsible for all the blood that was spilled." agreed Bervard to Philip's plan. Picking up what was left of Malvin's sword, he handed it to him and said, "hold on to your anger kid. I'll need it..., you'll need it for those responsible," and left their presence.

Bervard countenance was as one, who was lost in thoughts. Lost in emotions, regretting what it was he was seeing. As everyone else was puzzled as to what just happened, Philip spoke up, "that's the reason why I stepped down as king. And the reason why he seeks to get stronger. Bervard back then wanted war for what he saw. An emotional leader is never the best leader. Before our father died, I had him named Bervard as king instead, and I become general. Malvin, my word of advice to you is, to stay out of his way. The calm and collected king you saw leaving, is more dangerous now than you have ever known." Said Philip.

Indeed, this split change that occurred in Bervard was seen by everyone. Robert, among them all, was more taken back by it. The mental image he had of the king, was completely shattered. The king was living a life that was not his own only so he could cope with what he had seen these many years ago. Justifying the bloodshed with purpose and glory. The general was right to step down from the throne and take the head of the army. Looking at his general, Robert realized how fragile the king was. Maintaining authority and giving his men reasons to risk their lives versus taking it, was his way of preserving the lives of innocents.

"Dragon," spoke up Philip, "I leave the planning to you. My lieutenants will listen to you. But they will do things their way. The way they know will achieve greater success. It will take three days if I hurry now to get back to the castle to assemble our forces. I will split the troops and play decoy. Hopefully, we all make it back safely. Robert, John, Smith, Black, you must hold out until then. The king's safety is in your hands."

"General?" called out Robert as Philip was leaving. "I'd like to have Malvin with me. He more than proved his worth tonight." requested Robert.

Looking at Malvin, then at John and Smith, who nodded their approval, Philip agreed. "What about me?" asked Edwin.

"Messenger, you're with me. I have an important task for you, that you must not fail," said Philip as he dragged Edwin away. "You are to head west, towards the hills. My wife will no doubt be there waiting for me. Without fail, you are to take her and lead her away into the mountain chains and await further orders. Under no conditions are you to allow her to get back to the castle. Understood?" Ordered Philip.

"Crystal, sir," responded he, understanding the urgency of the matter.

Philip is to play decoy with the men with him, so the king and lieutenants could ride in the cover of the night into Serdio. If Bervard they are after, then dividing the troops puts every living soul and villages to the brink of annihilation by the coming enemy.

Tonight, was the night when war broke out. Tonight, was the night to survive to see the state of tomorrow. Tonight, and three other nights will determine the fate of Serdio. And tonight, Bervard had to resolve in his heart what he would do once he stood in the presence of Silas, king of Serdio.